Kiernan Kelly

In Bear Country
by Kiernan Kelly

In Bear Country

It was probably the smell of blood that drew the cougar.

A vicious-looking thing – it was a hundred and forty pounds of teeth, muscle, and meanness. Ears held flat against its head, its fangs were bared, its tail swishing from side to side as it growled menacingly at him. Pride felt his bowels loosen as he looked into its hungry, witchy green eyes.

Snarling, the cat's muscles bunched as it geared up to spring at Pride. A scream boiled up from his gut, ready to rip through his throat with what Pride was sure would be his last breath, when a single shot rang out and dropped the mountain lion dead in its tracks. One clean shot, straight through the bastard's mangy head.

Pride leaned back against the tree, his eyes drifting closed and his breath whooshing out of his lungs as relief washed over him like spring run-off down a mountainside. When he cracked them open again, he spotted his savior breaking through the brush just ahead.

Lordy, Pride didn't think he'd ever before seen a man so big. Wasn't just his height, although there was plenty of that. His chest was broad enough to fill out two ordinary men, three if they were on the scrawny side, like Pride. Wrapped in a bearskin cloak, the thick, shaggy black fur that spilled over his shoulders made him look even bigger, like he could've snapped Pride in two and used his leg bones to pick his teeth.

This is a work of fiction. Names, characters, places, and incidents either are the product of the author's imagination or are used fictitiously. Any resemblance to actual events, locales, organizations, or persons, living or dead, is entirely coincidental and beyond the intent of either the author or the publisher.

In Bear Country
TOP SHELF
An imprint of Torquere Press Publishers
PO Box 2545
Round Rock, TX 78680
Copyright © by Kiernan Kelly
Cover illustration by Rose Meloche
Published with permission
ISBN: 978-1-60370-007-8, 1-60370-007-2

www.torquerepress.com

All rights reserved, which includes the right to reproduce this book or portions thereof in any form whatsoever except as provided by the U.S. Copyright Law. For information address Torquere Press. Inc., PO Box 2545, Round Rock, TX 78680.
First Torquere Press Printing: April 2007
Second Printing: June 2008
Printed in the USA

If you purchased this book without a cover, you should be aware the this book is stolen property. It was reported as "unsold and destroyed" to the publisher, and neither the author nor the publisher has received any payment for this "stripped book".

**If you enjoyed In Bear Country,
you might enjoy these Torquere Press titles:**

In Bear Country II: The Barbary Coast by Kiernan Kelly

Latigo by BA Tortuga

Ranges by Dallas Coleman, Chris Owen, Julia Talbot and BA Tortuga

Redemption's Ride by BA Tortuga

Riding Heartbreak Road by Kiernan Kelly

In Bear Country

Chapter One

Ain't that always the way.

Seems like as soon as a man got his feet up under him, the earth would start to shaking and knock him right back down on his ass again.

Just once, Pride would have liked to see the sun come up with a dollar in his pocket and a roof of his own over his head. Hell, right now he'd settle for two bits and a broad-brimmed hat. 'Course, it never worked out that way. Every damn time he'd managed to pull his ass from the fire, God had seen fit to hold a lit match to his britches. This time was no different.

Truth was, Pride didn't hold much with God and figured that the feeling was mutual.

Pa would've had a jaw-full to say about that, Pride reckoned, but Pa was ten years in the ground and no doubt looking over God's shoulder, helping Him light the match. Although if Pride had his way, Pa would be roasting on a slow turning spit over the hottest fire in Hell instead.

Just fourteen when his father had died, his back sporting the scars of his old man's attempts to save his sorry soul, Pride had been scooped up, dressed in gray, handed a rifle, and pointed toward the North. Nobody asked him if he believed in the Cause. Hell, Pride was so wet behind the ears that he hadn't even figured out what the Cause *was* until the War was nearly over. Green and scared, he was lucky he hadn't shot his own damn foot off that first year.

He'd seen sights during the four years he'd fought in the War that no youngster should ever see, sights that still haunted his dreams from time to time. Men, or what used to be men before the cannonballs had ripped through them, lying on green fields soaked with crimson, crying out for their mothers. Blue or gray, black or white, it made no difference in Pride's eyes. Both sides had bled the same red. Women and children starving, walking with rags tied to their feet, burned out of their homes, their hollowed eyes cried dry. Entire families on the move, carrying their sick and dying with them, forced out by hunger or by stronger neighbors with bigger guns. The dead buried in shallow graves, or simply tossed to the side of the road, left to rot in the sun.

Pride had somehow managed to come through the War with his hide, if not his soul, intact -- dented and dinged but still covering his bones, only to get rounded up after the Surrender with the rest of his division and sent to the Rock Island prison camp for two years. Those two years were worse than any he'd ever lived before or since, including the four spent crawling on his belly in the mud, blood, and shit during the War.

What little food they'd been thrown was half-spoiled, the water fouled by livestock and men alike. Filth-covered, their uniforms worn until they were shredded and tattered into gray rags. Most had no shoes, their feet turning black with frostbite. Pride watched more men die when the cold came that first winter than he had in any skirmish he'd fought in. For a while it looked like Pride might join them, suffering as he had with a fever that hadn't cooled for days. The bullets and sabers had missed killing him, but the damned prison camp had near done him in.

When he'd been released from Rock Island with nothing but empty pockets and an emptier stomach, he'd wandered southwest. Living off the land as best he could, he'd snare a squirrel or a possum here and there, or a rabbit now and then. Got lucky once or twice noodling fish out of the water with his bare hands, but he went hungry more often as not. His bones poked up through his skin feeling sharper than a porcupine's quills. Still, he'd survived.

Eventually, Pride had found work riding fence for a rancher in Texas, working long and hard until both his fingers and his ass had sprouted blood blisters. Saved every nickel he could, buying nothing that he could do without – hadn't chawed tobacco or tasted nothing more refined than 'shine in years except at Christmas, and wore his pants and shirt until they weren't much more than holes strung together with thread. His coat had been worn through at the elbows, ragged at the bottom, and had only one button left. His hat had been beaten to hell and back, and wasn't much more than a misshapen lump atop his head. He did with what he had, and if he didn't have it, he did without. But after four years of pinching pennies, he'd managed to save enough in the grimy, rolled up sock he kept shoved inside his boot to buy a half-dead horse and a beat-up saddle, a rifle, a coat, a new hat, and hopefully, a better life.

Now this.

Pride turned his head and spat. Lord knew he didn't expect riches. Didn't expect nothing handed to him on a gleaming silver platter. Was willing to work hard and settle for a dry place to hang his hat. But just *once*, couldn't he manage to go a single, solitary day without getting tossed face-first into God's shit pile? Was that too much to ask?

He supposed he should count himself lucky that whoever had snuck up on his campsite in the dead of night, conked him over the head, stole Pride's horse, gun, hat, coat, and his dignity hadn't wanted to waste a bullet on him. Instead they'd tied him fast to a tree in the middle of the godforsaken foothills of the Colorado Rockies. Why, they'd even seen fit to leave him his boots. Grateful, that's what he should be – plum grateful.

The wind cut through him, as cold and as sharp as a knife. If he didn't manage to free himself soon, it wouldn't matter that the thieves hadn't killed him outright. He'd be dead just the same.

Trussed up to a young pine, the ropes chafed his wrists something fierce, and he could feel the sticky warmth of the blood on his hands as he rubbed them against the rough bark of the tree trying to saw himself loose. Pride figured that eventually he'd either cut through the ropes or his wrists, but either way it would free him. He surely hoped for the former, but wouldn't put the latter past his luck.

It was probably the smell of blood that drew the cougar.

A vicious-looking thing – it was a hundred and forty pounds of teeth, muscle, and meanness. Ears held flat against its head, its fangs were bared, its tail swishing from side to side as it growled menacingly at him. Pride felt his bowels loosen as he looked into its hungry, witchy green eyes.

Snarling, the cat's muscles bunched as it geared up to spring at Pride. A scream boiled up from his gut, ready to rip through his throat with what Pride was sure would be his last breath, when a single shot rang out and dropped the mountain lion dead in its tracks. One clean shot, straight through the bastard's mangy head.

Pride leaned back against the tree, his eyes drifting closed and his breath whooshing out of his lungs as relief washed over him like spring run-off down a mountainside. When he cracked them open again, he spotted his savior breaking through the brush just ahead.

Lordy, Pride didn't think he'd ever before seen a man so big. Wasn't just his height, although there was plenty of that. His chest was broad enough to fill out two ordinary men, three if they were on the scrawny side, like Pride. Wrapped in a bearskin cloak, the thick, shaggy black fur that spilled over his shoulders made him look even bigger, like he could've snapped Pride in two and used his leg bones to pick his teeth.

His shotgun was dwarfed in his meaty hands, looking like a child's plaything. But the bullet had done its job well enough. The cat lay still at Pride's feet, deader than last Sunday's chicken dinner.

"Much obliged," Pride said, nodding up at him. No sense in getting off on the wrong foot by sounding ungrateful. There was still the problem of being tied to a tree to get around, and Pride didn't want to put the man off while he still needed his help. 'Course, the man might be the one who'd knocked him a good one the night before and stolen everything he had to his name, but somehow Pride doubted it. This man didn't need to sneak around in the dark. He was big enough to walk up to a body in broad daylight and take what he wanted.

Dark blue eyes watched Pride from under shaggy brows. The man's features were nearly swallowed whole by an untrimmed, bushy beard that covered his face like a bird's nest. Exploding out from under his coonskin hat was a long, wild tangle of hair, thick and shiny black. He looked as feral as the damned cougar he'd just killed.

Pulling a wicked-looking Bowie from a sheath strapped

to one massive thigh, he reached down and sliced through the ropes that held Pride's hands tied to the tree. Pride's arms fell limply to his sides, as useless as two tits on a bull, completely numb from the hours they'd spent trussed up. Lordy, but they were gonna hurt like a sumbitch when the feeling came back to them.

"Name's Pride Falls," he said, wincing as he inspected his hands. Damn, but the rope had rubbed his wrists raw near to the bone. "Seems I owe you a debt of gratitude, Mister…?"

The big man cast an eye toward the sky, where the sun was beginning to sink behind the mountaintops. "Daylight's wasting."

"Pleased to meet you, Mr. Wasting."

"You got a smart mouth on you, boy."

"Yes sir, so I've been told. And it's 'bout near the only part of me that's smart. Lord knows my brain ain't but a half-step up from stupid, else I wouldn't have let myself get jumped," Pride smiled sheepishly.

At first Pride thought the man was growling, but he soon realized that it was a laugh that was rumbling around in his broad chest. Didn't sound like he laughed often, like he was rusty at it and still working out the kinks.

"Who tied you up, boy?"

"The same varmint that stole everything I owned. Didn't see him. Or them. Hit me while I was asleep. I come to trussed up like Aunt Mabel's Thanksgiving turkey." Pride was rewarded by another deep chuckle, this one sounding like it came easier than the first.

Bending to pick up one of the cat's hind legs, the man looked down at Pride, his beard twitching like he might have been smiling under all that hair. "You coming?" he asked as he wrenched the cougar up from the ground. He shouldered it as if it weighed no more than a goodly-sized mouse catcher, even though it must have weighed in at almost as much as Pride. The man was *strong*, and that was the gospel truth. "The sun's fixing to set and it gets cold mighty damn quick this high in the foothills. There's snow on the wind, too, and you don't look like you got enough fat on you to fry bacon, never mind keep warm."

"I'd be obliged, Mister… " Pride said, grinding his teeth and dragging himself to his feet. The pins and needles sensation he'd been feeling in his hands had deepened into an all out misery as the blood returned to them.

"Folks call me 'Bear'. Cabin's this way," the man said, turning and heading off into the scrub.

Pride followed behind him, Bear's body thankfully blocking the worst of the wind as they pushed on higher into the foothills of the Rocky Mountains. Twilight was upon them, casting the forest floor in shades of deepening gray by the time Pride spotted a neat and tidy log cabin set on a rise in a small clearing in the pines. Truthfully, it was none too soon. He'd kept his sore wrists tucked up tight under his armpits, but he was shivering fit to beat the band from the cold that had settled in as the sun had set.

His host dumped the carcass of the cougar on the ground outside the cabin and eased open the front door. Pride followed him inside, grateful to be out of the bitterly cold wind that was whistling through the trees. It was barely warmer inside the cabin than out, the hearth long gone cold, but at least there was no wind.

Bear flicked the head of a wooden match with his thumbnail, and used it to light an oil lamp. The soft yellow light made the pine walls of the cabin glow golden.

The inside of Bear's cabin was cozy, if spare. The raw

plank floors were scattered with pelts, deer mostly, with a few mountain lion mixed in. A small woodstove sat in one corner, a large, black iron skillet set on top. Cords of firewood were stacked neatly next to the large stone fireplace that sat at the back of the room. To the right of the hearth was a doorway that opened into a small alcove. Inside the tiny room, Pride could see a bed covered over with a colorful patchwork quilt.

A round, wooden tub sat to one side of the fireplace. Finishing off the furnishings of the cabin were a rough-hewn pine table, two chairs, and a tall cabinet. A few open shelves were nailed to the wall, holding bowls and baskets of various sizes. No curtains hung at the shuttered windows, just small pieces of hide tacked over them to keep out the draft; no dainty bric-a-brac stood on the mantle over the fireplace. The cabin itself smelled of wood smoke, tobacco, and man. *Bear was a bachelor, sure as skunks could squirt*, Pride thought.

Bear shrugged off his namesake cloak, and hung it and his coon hat neatly on a peg behind the door. Moving toward the hearth, he set about kindling a fire in the field stone fireplace. "Set yourself down, Pride. I'll boil us up some coffee," he rumbled, picking up a cast iron pot. He dipped it into a bucket of water that stood nearby, added coffee grounds scooped from a burlap bag that sat in the cabinet, then hung the pot on a hook over the flames. "What kind of a name is *Pride*, anyway?"

"My Pa was a preacher. I figure he was aiming for me to remember that Pride goeth before the fall, but that just goes to show you that the name don't make the man," Pride chuckled. "It was worse for my older brothers, Greed and Envy. If my Ma hadn't took sick and died before she could catch pregnant again, I figure he'd have gone for the whole set of the seven deadly sins. 'Course, it could've been worse. Could've named me Gluttony or

Lust, instead."

Bear laughed that deep-seated rumble again, and poked a stick in the fire, encouraging the flames to lick at the larger pieces of wood. "Where's your kin at now?"

"Dead. Pa died when I was fourteen. Heard both my brothers died during the first year of the War."

Bear shook his head. "Damn shame. War took a lot of good men."

"Yeah. And them that the War didn't take, the prison camps did."

"You fight in the War, Pride?"

"Yes sir, all four years, plus two in Rock Island. Just as soon forget all six of 'em, too. What about you, Bear? How'd you come by your name?"

Bear smirked. "My Christian name is Silas Davis, but nobody's called me that since the doctor smacked my ass and told my Ma she done birthed a bear instead of a boy."

Pride laughed, slapping his knee. "Stuck with it since you was born, huh? In your case the name fits, though."

"I reckon. Don't think on it much, really. It's just a name, and one's as good as another I suppose."

"Yup. Guess it don't matter none as long as it gets you called home to dinner. Where are your kinfolk, Bear?" Pride asked.

"Well, I'd best go skin that cat afore the snow starts," Bear said, striking a match and lighting another lantern. "Hope it ain't gonna be a big blow, but my knee's been spitting fire all day. Make yourself to home, and keep an eye on that coffee, Pride. I'll be back in directly."

When Bear opened the door and held up a lantern, Pride caught sight of a few fat, white flakes already beginning to sift down. He hadn't missed the fact that Bear hadn't answered him before he'd thrown his cloak over his shoulders and gone outside, closing the door behind him.

Releasing his breath in one long sigh, Pride reached between his legs and adjusted himself. There was something about Bear, something about his dark blue eyes and his large, strong body that made Pride's cock keep trying to sit up and beg. He turned his mind to the coffee, refusing to think on things better left unthunk.

Chapter Two

Bear's Bowie sawed through the cougar's hide like a hot knife through butter. After making a few necessary cuts through tendons and sinew, he slipped his hand under the skin, fisting and pulling and pushing until he'd removed it in nearly one piece from the carcass. He scraped the inner side clean of clinging bits of meat and fat, then rolled it up tight, sticking it in an iron box near the front door. It would freeze solid, and would keep if the snow got so deep that Bear couldn't dig it out until spring to tan it.

Hacking at the skinned carcass, Bear removed as much fat as he could easily reach. He dragged the rest of the beast as far from the cabin as he thought necessary. Wolves and whatnot would make short work of it. He didn't need the meat. He had more than enough elk, beaver, squirrel, rabbit, and possum -- some dried, some fresh -- set by that he didn't have to worry about food for the winter. Besides, the cat would taste like shit anyway. But he'd render the cougar's fat into tallow for candles.

Walking around the side of the cabin, Bear checked his smokehouse. The small outbuilding was set back from the cabin, far enough away to keep the worst of the smoke from getting inside the house, and keep the risk of fire to a minimum. It might be best to transfer the rest of the meat into the larder while he was still able. The snow was falling heavier already, and it wouldn't be the first time that an early blizzard had blown in, leaving him snowbound.

Stranger or no, Bear couldn't bring himself to leave Pride to wander the foothills with no coat and no supplies. Full dark would have been on him afore long, bringing with it the bitter cold of night and the snow that had been threatening all day. It would have been kinder to snap his neck rather than turn him loose. He'd had no choice but to bring Pride home with him, but if it snowed too deep then Pride would be snowbound along with Bear.

With an extra mouth to feed, Bear reckoned he'd best be prepared. Especially since Pride was so scrawny he looked like a good strong breeze would blow him clear to Mexico. Boy didn't look like he'd eaten more than a handful of nothing in as many days. It took Bear several trips, but he'd finally stuffed the larder full, squeezing the last hunk of smoked venison in and closing the lid on the large, wooden bin. Piled with heavy stones, the lid would keep animals out of his cache.

The larder was his own invention, one he was rightly proud of, an idea that had come to him after he'd nearly starved to death his first winter in the mountains. He'd laid enough meat by in a stone-covered cairn, but hadn't been able to reach it through the deep snow until it had been almost too late. If it hadn't been for dried strips of jerky he'd stored inside the cabin, he'd most likely have starved to death before the snow had melted enough for him to dig out his supplies.

First, he'd dug down deep into the cold, hard earth, lining the pit with stones, before building a wooden box with a tight-fitting lid on top of it. He'd cut a small hole in the side of his cabin that opened into the larder, making the meat easy to reach even in the dead of winter when the snows piled high against the windows and door. A heavy piece of bearskin, hung fur side facing the hole, served him the same way it had served the bear it had once covered. Kept the heat inside the cabin and the cold outside in the larder. The meat would stay frozen, supplementing his store of dried venison.

He kept one largish piece of venison out. A nice hot roast with some of the beans he'd put up last season would fill their bellies. With the coffee, it would make for a good supper. Lord knew Pride looked like he could use one. The boy was about as scrawny as the smallest runt of a sickly litter.

Looked young enough to still be sucking on his mama's teat, for that matter. Pride's beard wasn't more than a dusting on his jaw, and although his eyes were hollowed, his skin was a smooth as a baby's rear end. Bear would have put him at much younger than he was, if Pride hadn't told him he'd served all four years in the War, plus the two in that prison camp. He had to be twenty-four or twenty-five years old. Still a heap younger than Bear, but a lot older than Bear would have pegged him for.

Towheaded was how Bear's Ma would have described Pride's pale yellow hair. It reminded Bear of the color of his Pa's corn after the ears had been picked and husked. His eyes were dark brown, his skin sun-bronzed. He had a quick smile, but it was a guarded one, much like Bear's own.

There was something about Pride that Bear couldn't quite put his finger on. Nothing bad – Bear had a touch of *The Gift*, as his Ma had always called it, knowing good folk from bad from the moment he set eyes on them. Bear always trusted his gut, and right now it was telling him that Pride was a good man. There was something different about him, though, something he was hiding. Bear could see that right off. Been through a hard time, from the looks of him, too. Bear could see it in the dark smudges under his brown eyes. Had eyes like a whipped hound dog, Pride did, sad and hopeful, but just a tiny bit wary at the same time. Like he was praying that the hand holding out the bone wasn't just a distraction from the boot that was fixing to kick him.

Bear broke through a thin skin of ice that covered the water in a bucket he kept near the larder, washing his hands and rinsing off the meat. Looking up at the sky, he blinked away snowflakes that clung to his eyelashes. Yup, those clouds were belly-full of snow, he reckoned. Gonna dump a goodly amount before she blew herself out.

By the time Bear re-entered the cabin, carrying his hunk of fresh-smoked meat, Pride had found two cups, one tin and the other chipped china, and was lifting the tin pot carefully from its hook over the fire. The rich smell of strong coffee filled the cabin as he poured the steaming, black liquid into the cups.

"Smells good. Always did like my coffee strong," Bear said. He picked up a long metal rod and skewered the hunk of venison, then suspended the spit over the fire. "Ain't got no cream but I got a little sugar, if you want it sweet."

"I'd be obliged, if you can see your way clear to spare a dab or two."

Bear hung up his cloak and lifted down a canister from the top shelf of the cabinet. Adding a bit of sugar to both their cups, he stirred his, then handed Pride the spoon. Sipping the scalding hot liquid, Bear smiled as it warmed his belly. "Nothing like good hot coffee to warm a man from the inside out."

"Truer words ain't never been spoken," Pride agreed, blowing across the rim of his cup before taking a swallow.

"So, you was going to tell me where your kinfolk are, Bear," he said, wincing a bit. The coffee must have burned his tongue, no matter that he'd blown on it first.

Bear eyed him over his coffee cup, sipping slowly. Might as well get it over with. Lying had never sat well with Bear, and not answering a direct question was about the same thing in his book. The Sin of Omission, his ma had called it. "Dead. My Pa had a little farm over near Abilene, nothing much, just a few acres but enough to keep us all fed. Rancher who owned the land next to ours came in looking to buy my Pa out, but he wasn't selling. I was over in town getting coffee and flour for my Ma when it happened. Came home, found them all dead -- every last one of them. My parents, my brothers, even my baby sister. Bastard shot her in her cradle. My pa had the rancher's brand burned onto his forehead."

"Oh, shit, Bear...I'm sorry," Pride said, setting his cup down.

"No need. Wasn't you that killed them," Bear said. "But I thank you."

"What did you do?"

"Got my daddy's rifle, saddled up a horse, and went after the rancher. Killed the sorry sumbitch as he sat on his front porch, laughing at me with a handful of his men. Guess he figured I wouldn't pull the trigger in front of witnesses. He was wrong. Shot him right in his lying mouth. Killed two of his men, too. Didn't want to, but it was them or me. Took a bullet in my arm, but it passed clean through."

"That why you're up here? You got the law after you?" Pride asked.

"Yup. I'm a wanted man, I reckon. Rancher had money, friends in Abilene. Sheriff was a good man, though. Knew me my whole life. Said he believed me, but he said that the brand wasn't proof that the rancher had killed my family. There was a handful of men saw *me* shoot him and his men, though. Told me to hightail it out and not to ever come back. Found my way here, and built this cabin. Been here ever since."

"How long has it been, Bear?"

"Don't rightly know. A double-handful of years or more, I reckon. Didn't really see a need to keep track." He got up and walked to the hearth, hunkering down to turn the spit. The flames jumped and sputtered as fat from the roast dripped down into the fire.

"Why head up here? Why not someplace warmer, like down by the Gulf of Mexico? Or better still, out to California? That's where I'm headed. Nice warm beaches, all that gold folks been finding out there... "

Bear bit his lip, watching Pride's face carefully. There was something about him that made Bear trust him. Something that told Bear that Pride wouldn't laugh at him like other folk had laughed at his Pa.

"I got something I brought with me, something I got from my Pa," he said. He heaved his bulk up from the hearth and went into the alcove. Searching under the bed, he brought out a small wooden box and set it on the table. "It's the only thing I took when I left, 'cept for my horse and my guns. Horse up and died a few years back, but I still got my guns and this," he said, opening the lid.

Inside the box lay a battered black Bible. "The Bible was my Ma's," he said, running his fingers over the grainy leather of the cover. The gilded lettering had long worn off, but he remembered her holding it as he sat at her feet while she read her favorite passages to her children. His Ma had always been partial to the Twenty-third Psalm, and when Bear lifted the cover the book fell open to that passage. Nestled between the vellum pages was a folded, aged piece of thin buckskin.

He took it out, carefully spreading it open on the

table before Pride. "It's a map my Pa got from an old fur trapper. Saved his life from snakebite once, and the man gave my Pa this in return. Said it was a treasure map. Pa never got around to searching for it, but I figured I had nothing better to do."

"Treasure? What kind of treasure, Bear?"

"Don't know. Ain't found it yet."

"But the map is of these foothills?"

"Yeah. The trapper told my Pa that this was area. See here?" Bear said, pointing to a crude drawing of snake in the lower left hand corner of the map. His finger moved over the buckskin to the upper right hand corner. "I figure that to be Snake Creek. That puts the 'X' somewhere here, up in these foothills. But I ain't been able to figure out these other squiggly marks he done drew on here yet."

"Ain't that something," Pride said, nodding his head. "Could be a treasure map at that. That there looks kind of like a skull, don't it?" Pride said, pointing to a circular black spot near the center of the map. "Eyeholes and all. Mind if I have another cup of coffee? The first slid down so good, it's wanting company."

Bear smiled and nodded. He'd been right. Pride hadn't laughed at him. Bear was never wrong about people. He held out his own cup for Pride to refill, saying, "Pa used to take it out and study on it at night. Folks thought my Pa was foolish to believe in it. Said it was a waste of time."

"Don't seem foolish to me. It's a map, ain't it? Folks don't make maps for no reason. Must lead to somewhere or something."

Bear nodded, gently re-folding the buckskin and sticking it back inside the Bible. Returning the book to the box and the box to its hiding place under his bed, he walked back into the main room and cracked open the front door.

Immediately, a strong, bitter gust of wind swept inside,

fanning the flames in the fireplace. "Shit, it's working itself up to be a humdinger outside. Looks like maybe you might be staying here for a while, Pride."

"I'm truly sorry to be a burden to you, Bear. You've been more than kind, and that's a fact. Maybe I should leave now, afore you get stuck with me. I don't have no way to repay you for what you done for me already. Those bastards stole everything I had in the world." Pride said, standing up and looking toward the door.

"You just set your scrawny butt back down, Pride. Ain't going to turn you out to wander into the storm. Truth is, I'm enjoying the company. Been alone since I left the homestead. It's good to have a body to talk to. When the storm blows itself out we can go hunting to replace the meat, if it'll make you feel better. I got plenty put by, but I reckon you could do with some supplies."

"There's a special place in Heaven waiting for you, Bear," Pride said as he sat down again. The shimmer in his eyes told Bear it had been a long while since he'd last been shown a kindness.

Lifting his cup, Bear smiled. "Well, here's to hoping that it waits a good long while afore I get there to claim it."

Chapter Three

Levi swore softly under his breath as the crick in his neck shot up over the back of his skull, threatening to develop into an all out skull-buster of a headache.

The storm had raged through the night and half the morning, the wind a-blowing and a-wailing fit to wake the dead. The patched-up tent they'd hastily pitched in the lee of a rock overhang wasn't big enough for two men, let alone three, and sleep had been damn near impossible. If an elbow wasn't poking Levi in the gut, then a knee was jamming him in the small of the back. Not to mention that the two men he was bunked in with both smelled worse than a hog's backside.

The snow was near a foot deep as far as Levi could tell when he'd first gotten up and crawled over the two of them, cracking open the front flap of the tent. Snow had been falling so thick that he could barely see the horses that were tethered next to their tent under the overhang. He'd ducked back inside, shivering from the cold, and it had seemed he'd just managed to fall back asleep when Zack's elbow had jabbed him a good one in his gut. He woke up coughing and gasping for air.

"Get up, you lazy bags of shit! It's stopped snowing, and daylight's a-wasting."

A weak sun was peeking though the clouds. Judging by its position high in the sky, Levi figured it was nearing noon when the three men crawled out from the tent, each twisting his spine to work out the kinks. Tramping through the snow, Jeb went to tend to the horses while Levi saw to a fire and put on the makings for coffee.

The trail they'd been following would be lost under the fresh powder and Levi knew that fact was going to have Zack Jensen so riled up he was like as not to shoot a man as look at him. Ornery as a pole cat in the best of times, he was going to be downright hateful now that nature had spat on his plans. It had been Zack's idea that had them wandering the foothills at a time of year most other men – at least those with half a brain -- were bunkered down in town with a bottle of whiskey and a warm bed, waiting on the spring thaw. Problem was, a smart man didn't say *no* to Zack, lest he wanted a gutful of lead for breakfast.

So instead of holing up in a room with a hot fire and warm whore, they'd been huddled inside a leaky tent on the cold, hard ground, freezing their asses off, and waiting out the storm.

"Maybe we'd best head back down into St. Elmo now that it's cleared, Zack. Ain't never gonna track him with fresh snow on the ground." Jeb said, walking over to the small campfire with a small, tin flask of rockgut in his hand. He took a long swallow then passed it over to Levi.

Levi kept his eye on Zack as he drank. He'd been riding with Zack for nearly fifteen years, and knew his moods almost better than he knew his own. They'd met up in Abilene shortly after Zack's daddy had been killed. Levi, living hand-to-mouth, fresh out of jail for knocking the front teeth out of a man he'd suspected of cheating at cards, and with no prospects for the future, had thrown his lot in with Zack. They'd lived mostly outside the law, true enough, but they hadn't been caught yet and likely never would. Still, Levi had learned quick when to duck and cover around Zack. Jeb, on the other hand, had only been with them for a few weeks and hadn't yet learned to keep his jaw still when Zack got that mean look in his eye.

"No telling that he's even alive. Maybe he got caught in the storm and froze to death," Jeb continued, wiping his mouth on the sleeve of his new coat. He'd won the coat in a coin toss, but Levi didn't begrudge him it. After all, Levi had won that fella's shotgun, nearly new and not a scratch on the barrel. 'Course, Zack had gotten his horse, and hadn't had to flip them for it, neither.

It was pure luck that they'd stumbled across that man fast asleep like he was, all alone out in the open. Didn't take much to slam him upside the head with a rock and tie him up. They'd left him for dead, taking whatever they wanted from him, right down to his coat and hat.

Zack took what Zack wanted. Always had, and always would. That's just the way it was, and anyone who knew him learned quick not to cross him. Which was why Levi didn't argue with Zack over the horse. Levi wasn't eager to get a bullet planted between his eyes or a hatchet buried in his skull while he was sleeping.

That Zack had a mean streak was an understatement if Levi had ever heard one. He'd left that man alive and trussed up like a Christmas present for the wind and the wolves out of sheer cruelty. A kinder man would've put a bullet in his head.

Levi bit his tongue and busied himself pouring coffee. Jeb was walking on thin ice, and didn't even see it cracking under his feet.

Zack narrowed his eyes at Jeb. "He's alive. He's been living up here for years. Knows these hills too well to get caught unprepared. We're close – I can smell it. It if wasn't for the storm we would've had him by now."

"Maybe it ain't even real, Zack. Ever think of that? Could be he was lying about the map." Levi could see the black storm clouds gathering in Zack's eyes as Jeb pressed his point, and winced.

"It's real. Big man like that don't need to make up stories for attention. Besides, I heard from that old man, Watterman, down at the saloon, that he seen the map with his own eyes the first year Bear come through St. Elmo's. Laughed in Bear's face and told him he was asking for an early grave to go trekking up the mountain on a fool's errand."

"That don't mean that the map's real, just 'cause Bear's stupid enough to believe in it."

"It's real. A man don't spend fifteen years up in these mountains searching for something that ain't real."

"That don't mean nothing, Zack. He ain't found the treasure yet, has he? Makes a man believe that it don't exist." Christ on toast, Jeb was looking for a swift boot to heaven. Levi took a half-step away from him, just in case Zack's aim was off.

"Yeah? Well, *I* believe in it. I'm gonna get that map and there ain't gonna be enough of Bear left to feed the crows when I'm done with him. I've been hunting his ass for too long to give up now. You want out?" Zack growled, baring yellowed, tobacco-stained teeth at Jeb. Without warning, a hard fist swung out and caught Jeb on his bearded jaw. He was down and looking stunned before he even knew he'd been hit, the long barrel of Zack's revolver pointed right between his eyes.

Levi shook his head, averting his eyes. The only way out of this was in a shallow grave, and he knew it. That was mostly why he was still with the badger after fifteen years. You didn't cross Zack. Ever.

Jeb went pale as he sat rubbing his jaw and looking a bullet in the eye. "N-no, Zack. I was just wondering, is all."

"Don't. I owe Bear. Done spent fifteen years of my life tracking him and I ain't about to let him slip through my fingers now just because a snot-nosed kid like you is afraid of a little snow."

"I ain't afraid, Zack," Jeb lied.

Levi wanted to laugh. Jeb was plenty afraid – of Zack.

"Good. Then shake a leg and get moving. We're gonna head up to that summit," Zack said, pointing to a sheer outcrop several hundred feet above where they stood. "Should be able to see most of the valley from there. If Bear's cabin is anywhere nearby, we'll see the smoke from his fire."

Pride spent the night curled up in a nest of warm furs laid down in front of the fireplace. Banked to last the night, the fire's heat and his full belly had lulled him to sleep in no time flat. For the first time in a long time, Pride didn't dream of the War, or of his Pa, or any of the other hardships he'd suffered over the years. He'd slept the sleep of the angels, as his Ma used to say.

He awoke to the smell of strong coffee and flapjacks, blinking his eyes open to see Bear fussing at the kitchen table. Pride surely must have slept like the dead for him not to hear Bear messing with the pots and pans over the small woodstove. The man was making more noise than a buffalo stampede.

Sitting up, he rubbed his hands over his face, groggily. "Should've woke me up, Bear. Didn't aim to sleep so long."

"You was sleeping deep. Figured you needed it."

"That I did. I'm obliged, Bear."

"Don't think on it. Get up and have some breakfast. My flapjacks are more like bricks than food, but I got some honey to go on top."

"Smells real good, Bear," Pride smiled. He tried not to notice that Bear hadn't bothered to put on the red flannel shirt he'd been wearing the day before, and how his woolens clung to the muscles of his shoulders and arms that strained at the gray fabric. There wasn't an ounce of spare fat on Bear – he was all solid muscle.

The deep vee of the neckline of his underwear showed silky black hair curling over his chest, his skin glistening with drops of sweat raised by the heat of the stove. When he lifted the heavy skillet up, flipping the flapjacks in the air, biceps near as large around as Pride's head bulged, and Pride couldn't help but wonder what those massive arms would feel like wrapped around him.

His groin tightened pleasantly, and he quickly turned away from Bear lest he see what had raised up in Pride's britches. He tried to clear his mind, trying to concentrate of the homey smell of the johnnycakes and coffee.

Standing up, Pride stretched, then folded and piled the hides he'd slept on over the stack of cordwood near the fireplace. Walking toward the front door of the cabin, he took another deep breath, as if trying to wake himself up by just *smelling* the aroma of strong coffee in the air.

"Where are you going?" Bear asked. The frying pan sizzled as he laid a thick hank of smoked bacon on it to fry.

Pride paused with his hand on the peg that held the door closed, ready to slide it free of its bolt-hole. "Just need to pee, Bear. Back in a minute."

"Best to use the bucket. Storm ain't over yet."

Groaning, Pride cracked open the front door. A thick, silently falling curtain of white was on the other side, and the wind swept cold powder in over his bare feet. "Shit," he said, dancing the snow off his feet and closing the door, "ain't it *ever* gonna stop?"

Bear chuckled. "Eventually, I reckon. Bucket's in the corner. Hurry now, breakfast is almost ready."

They sat at the square pine table, two tin plates piled with more flapjacks and bacon than Pride could hope to eat in a week. His stomach rumbled, reminding him that it had been a good long while since his last meal, and that had been skimpy and tasteless. Digging in, he slowed down to appreciate the hearty taste of the thick flapjacks and sweet honey, and the smoky flavor of the bacon.

"This is mighty good, Bear. Damn good," Pride said, lifting another forkful of flapjacks to his mouth. He ate until his sides bulged, feeling like he was about to bust a seam. Couldn't remember the last time he'd eaten as much, when he'd last felt truly and well fed.

He watched Bear with fascination as Bear put away the mound of food that covered his plate, cleaning it down to the tin while barely taking a breath between bites.

Lordy, but that man had an appetite. Stood to reason though. He was nearly as big as a house. Needed lots of fuel to stoke that furnace, Pride reckoned. He grinned and pushed his plate, still bearing a half-stack of cakes and a goodly-sized piece of bacon on it, toward Bear. "I can't eat another bite, Bear. I'm stuffed full to bursting. Shame to let it go to waste, though."

"Ain't nothing goes to waste in *my* house," Bear grinned, pulling the plate towards himself and digging in. Pride smiled, watching him eat it down to crumbs. He was almost surprised when Bear didn't lick the plate clean.

After the plates and skillet had been scraped, washed,

and dried, Bear dragged his chair over to the hearth. Selecting a small piece of wood, he took out his Bowie knife and started whittling, whistling a tune as thin curls of wood fell in a shower, piling up around his feet. *Red River Valley*, Pride thought it was, humming along under his breath.

He wandered over to the open shelves near the cupboard, his eyes alighting on a shelf low to the ground that was piled with small wooden figures. Animals abounded – wolves, horses, bear, deer, and the like. There were tiny log cabins and barns, and an entire steam engine carved from hard pine. Picking it up, Pride ran his fingers over the smooth wood. Each tiny wheel and piston, the smokestack, cab, and tender had been sculpted in perfect detail. Took a heap of patience and a load of talent to cut something so fine from a hunk of wood.

His eyes flicked over to Bear, his bulk settled comfortably in the sturdy wooden chair, his long legs stretched out in front of him toward the fire, his ankles crossed, as he slowly stripped another long, thin curl from the hunk of pine in his hand. His hands were big and his fingers thick, and it amazed Pride that Bear could coax something as beautiful and fragile as the locomotive out of a hard piece of wood. The carvings gave Pride new insight into Bear's character.

"You make all these, Bear?" He asked, indicating the locomotive in his hands.

"Yeah. Got to do something to pass the time. Made lots more than that over the years, but I burned most of 'em during the winters."

"Shame to burn things as nice as these. You're a real artist, that's what you are. Like as not, you could sell these. Make yourself some money."

"Who'd spend good money on whimsies like these?" Bear laughed. "Sometimes when I got to go down to town to get supplies, I bring a bagful with me to St. Elmo's and pass 'em out to the schoolchildren."

"That's real generous of you, Bear."

Bear shrugged, but Pride could see a flush heat his cheeks. Pride pulled his own chair up to the fire, got a knife from the cupboard and pulled a piece of wood from the stack. Without a word, he began chipping tiny flakes from it, imitating Bear. 'Course, *his* carving probably wouldn't resemble nothing more than a chopped up piece of wood, but Bear was right – whittling was as fine a way as any to pass the time.

By early afternoon the storm had blown itself out. A pristine blanket of white that was a foot deep in most places and nearing three feet in drifts covered the hills, absorbing sound and glistening brightly in the sun.

Bear gave him an old coat fashioned from the hide of an elk to replace the one he'd lost to the thieves. The fur was heavy, smoky, and big enough for two men the size of Pride, but it was warm and Pride was as grateful as a man could get.

"I got some traps I want to check afore the next storm blows in," Bear said, as they stood calf-deep in the snow in front of the cabin. "Could use your help, unless you're wanting to start out now. If we find 'em full, you can have the meat if you want it. I don't need it none."

"I'm obliged again, Bear, and I'd be pleased to help," Pride answered. The man had saved his life, given him food and shelter and a coat. The least he could do was check a few traps before taking off for parts unknown. Not to mention that the prospect of having some provisions, no matter how little, made his survival seem a bit more likely.

Truth was, Pride wasn't in any particular hurry to go anywhere. He had no money, no gun, no supplies other than what Bear might find in his traps, and no horse to carry him. He sure as shit couldn't risk trying to make it over the mountains without them. It was looking like he was going to have to turn his sorry ass straight around and head back to Texas, maybe get his old job back from Mr. Halloway. The thought was daunting. It burned his butt and soured his stomach thinking on the way he was going to have to beg. Halloway was a hateful old coot with a mean streak a country mile wide. He had a way of making a man feel two feet tall, and Pride wasn't looking forward to having to face him after quitting like he done.

'Course, he'd only have to worry about begging for his job if he survived tramping down through the foothills in the snow. The cold was bad enough but the wolves were a helluva lot worse, and the foothills had plenty of both. Plus, once he came down out of the hills, he'd still have a month or more of hard walking out of Colorado, and across parts of the New Mexico Territory and Texas to reach the ranch.

And that was only if another storm didn't come howling down off the mountains and bury him alive in a frigid, white grave.

Now that he thought on it, begging Halloway for his job back was the least of his worries. Pride was seriously doubtful that he'd be alive long enough for it to come to that.

"See that hollow over yonder?" Bear asked, bringing Pride's thoughts back from his troubles.

"Yeah, I see it. What of it, Bear?"

"Shot me a grizzly right there last summer."

"That a fact? A grizzly?"

"Yup. Big fucker, too. Must've been eight feet on its hind legs. I was setting these snares and suddenly there he was, coming at me fast from that hollow. Must have had his den there. That's one thing you need to remember about this land, Pride – it's bear country. They own it, lock, stock, and barrel. Ain't nothing alive that can take on a full-grown bear, except a bullet in the head. And that don't even stop 'em quick enough sometimes."

"No shit? Ain't never seen a grizzly afore. Seen black bear, sure enough, but no grizzlies."

"They're twice the size of a black bear. But it's the females you got to really watch out for. They're smaller than the males but three times as ornery when they've got their cubs with them. They'll be hibernating this time of year, birthing their cubs in early spring. But still, it's best that you keep your eyes peeled when you're out in the wood around these parts."

"I will. Thanks, Bear," Pride said, mentally adding 'grizzly' to the list of things that might kill him before spring. Warily, he peered into the hollow as they passed it, shuddering as he imagined a giant of a bear, fangs dripping, charging at him from out of the darkness.

He followed Bear up deep into the foothills, stopping every so often to dig through the snow to reveal a trap or snare Bear had set. Several were full, and both men had a brace of rabbit and a couple of squirrel slung over his shoulder by the time they were done.

Chapter Four

It was late afternoon by the time they'd hiked back to Bear's cabin.

"Thinking maybe it might be best for you to stay another night, Pride. It's late, and full dark will be on you afore you can get too far," Bear said. He swept the snow clear from a small area in front of the cabin and set to work skinning the animals they'd brought back with them.

"Don't want to be a burden, Bear," Pride answered, although he knew Bear was right. Trying to get back to the ranch at this time of year with no weapons or supplies was dangerous enough, but to leave at this hour with night falling was just plain suicide. "You done enough for me already. But again, I'd be in your debt."

"Don't even think on it. Go inside and grab a knife from the cupboard. I can use your help skinning these varmints."

Four hands made short work of the animals Bear had trapped, their hides cleaned and rolled and added to the cougar's in the metal box, their meat cut into small, tongue-shaped pieces and strung near the fire inside the cabin to dry. Bones and other inedible parts were hauled out into the forest for the carrion eaters to feast on. Nature's way of cleaning house, was how Pride always thought of the vultures, rodents, and other creatures that would be happy to get such an easy meal, especially with snow on the ground.

Both men were sweating by the time they'd finished, even though the temperature had dropped again. The wind blew even colder, the skies graying with thick ominous clouds scudding across the sky, blocking out the setting sun. Another storm was in the making, blowing in from the west across the jagged mountaintops of the Rockies.

Heading inside, they stripped out of their outer clothes, both hurrying to stand near the fire to warm up. After a while, Bear turned to Pride. "Mind a cold supper tonight? I got strips of jerky, hardtack, and some put-ups from last season. Beets, and some apples I put by. And coffee, of course."

"That'll be fine, Bear," Pride smiled, rubbing his hands over the fire, warming them. They felt near frozen stiff, but the heat from the crackling flames soothed the cold away soon enough.

Bear picked up a bucket and went outside, returning a moment later with it brimming full with snow. He set it near the fire to melt. "No offense, Pride, but you and me reek. Figure a nice warm bath would do us both a heap of good." He nodded toward the large, round tub that sat in a corner between the woodstove and the hearth.

"A bath? Um…don't you think that'll use up a lot of firewood? Heating all that water, I mean," Pride stammered. The last thing he wanted was to get naked in front of Bear, especially since getting an eyeful of Bear out of his long johns was likely to give Pride a problem he wouldn't be able to hide.

"Nah, I got plenty. All this in here, plus I got half the

forest stacked up under that window," Bear answered. "Besides, my knee is a pure misery right now, and hot water always soothes it nicely."

It took several trips for more snow, each newly melted bucketful carefully poured into a pot suspended over the fire to warm, but soon the tub was half-filled with steaming water. Bear stripped out of his boots and clothes and slipped into the water with a long, drawn-out, contented sigh. "Hauled this tub up on my back during one of my first trips down off the mountain for supplies. Traded a dozen of my best pelts for it. Best trade I ever made, and that's a fact."

Pride set about getting the fixings out for their dinner, setting the table and taking down the mason jars of beets and apples. He fidgeted, trying to keep himself occupied, trying not to think about Bear naked and wet in the tub. It didn't work, but at least his hands were busy. He made sure to keep his back to Bear whenever possible, trying to hide the hard bulge that had risen up at his crotch. With any luck, Pride might be able to put off his own bath until after Bear had gone to bed.

"Pride, fetch me that quilt off my bed, if you don't mind."

Pride winced, but did as Bear had asked. He returned from the alcove with Bear's quilt piled in his arms just as Bear heaved himself out of the tub.

Pride's eyes widened as they took in the sight of Bear, naked and dripping, reaching for the quilt as he stepped over the side of the tub.

At least six foot three, Bear was a mountain of a man, and his body was honed to perfection by the hard life he led. Each muscle was sharply defined, bulging with unconscious strength. His chest was covered with soft black hair, plastered to his skin in swirling patterns from his bath. A line of hair led down the center of his chiseled stomach to a thick thatch of short curls between his legs. His cock was flaccid but impressive nonetheless, long and thick. His thighs -- rock-hard and each as big around as both of Pride's put together -- and his strong calves were dusted with hair. Standing sideways as he shook out the quilt, Bear's ass was as firm as the rest of him, two perfectly curved globes. Bear's midnight blue eyes met Pride's briefly as he caught Pride staring, unspoken questions flickering in them.

Pride wrenched his eyes away and sat at the table, fiddling with a strip of jerky as Bear walked over and sat down. He could feel his face burning, worrying whether Bear was going to call him on staring at him like he'd been. Wasn't right for one man to look at another like that, but Pride couldn't help himself. Truth be told, he didn't want to either. He'd *liked* looking at Bear, and it was all he could do to keep from looking again, to keep from trying to see under the patchwork that Bear had wrapped around himself.

To his relief, Bear didn't say a word about it. Just picked up a strip of dried jerky and bit into it. "Mind putting water on for coffee, Pride? I'll empty the tub and heat more water up for your bath after we eat."

Pride nodded, flicking his eyes up toward Bear. Bless him, but the man didn't look like he was going to say a word about the way Pride had been looking at him. Either he was more of an innocent than Pride had imagined, or more forgiving than any man he'd met before. Swallowing hard, Pride got busy making the coffee, trying not to let on that parts of him had gotten painfully hard from seeing all of Bear's fine flesh.

He lingered as long over supper as he could, hoping that Bear would get drowsy enough to say goodnight and leave him to bathe in private. Unfortunately, directly after he'd stuffed the last slice of apple into his mouth, Bear had dressed in a pair of dry long-johns – giving Pride another good, long look at his fine rear end, which hadn't helped Pride's problem in the least -- and had started heating water for Pride's bath.

Sighing, Pride went to help him, scooping buckets of dirty bath water out of the tub and chucking them out the front door, until the tub was empty and ready to be filled again. He watched the water rise bucketful by bucketful, dreading the moment that was coming.

"Bear, why don't you go get some sleep? I can finish up in here – clean up the supper dishes, I mean. I'll take my bath when I'm through," Pride said, trying to keep his voice from sounding strained.

"Ain't tired yet. Thought I'd whittle a while before turning in. Go on now, the dishes can wait, the water won't. It'll get cold." Bear nodded toward the bath, then fetched his knife and the carving he'd started that morning. Settling himself down by the fire, he began chipping carefully at the piece of wood.

Pride had no choice but to strip down. He kept his back to Bear, uncharacteristically quiet as he unbuttoned his grayed long johns. Lordy, how he didn't want to do this, and wished he could think of an excuse that might get him out of it. He'd tried, but Bear wasn't having any of it. It wasn't his back that he was hesitant to uncover. It was his front - namely, the hard-on that was trying to poke itself free through the crotch of his long johns. Fully dressed, he'd been able to keep his arousal hidden, crossing his legs or keeping his back toward Bear whenever his body had chosen to betray him by sending his groin the signal to stand up and be counted.

But there was no way to hide it if he had to strip down bare-ass naked. His dick would poke out straight and ready and just as hard to miss as one of the tall pines that dotted the foothills. His only hope was to hold his long johns up in front of him until he could manage to slip into the tub.

Pulling his shoulders free from the sleeves of his long johns, he froze as he heard Bear suck his breath in between his teeth. The scars. Damn. He'd almost forgotten they were there.

"Holy Sweet Christ, Pride..." Bear whispered. He stood up and stepped close enough that Pride could smell Bear's scent – spicy and clean, and feel Bear's warm breath against the cool skin of his back. "Who did this to you? This happen while you was in prison? Those Yankee bastards... "

"Wasn't the Yankees. It was my Pa," Pride answered, swallowing hard and twisting the wool of his long johns in his hands.

"Your own *pa* did that? Lord, Pride – he must've laid you open to the bone to leave them scars."

"Yeah, he did."

"Why? What did you do?"

"Got caught doing something I shouldn't a-been, something real bad. 'Specially bad for a preacher's boy." The memory still tasted bitter on Pride's tongue, even after all the years that had passed since.

"What could you have done that would make a man do this to his own flesh and blood?" Bear asked.

"Something that he thought was gonna damn my soul straight to Hell."

"You kill a man?" Pride fought a shiver as Bear's thick finger lightly traced one of the many long scars that laced the flesh of Pride's back.

"No. Not directly, anyway."

"Not directly? How's a body kill a man *indirectly*?"

"It was my fault that he died. He didn't deserve what they done to him, neither. He was a good man, a kind man. But when Pa came in the barn and found us, he..."

Pride's voice cracked, and he lost his battle to keep from shivering. But it was no longer a shiver of pleasure from Bear's touch, but one of remembered pain and hate and rage.

"He what? What was you doing that was so terrible, Pride?" Bear asked softly. "Oh..." His breath expelled in a rush against Pride's back. "I see. Your pa caught you two..."

"Yeah, he did," Pride hissed over his shoulder. "Okay? You satisfied now, Bear? I ain't like other men. I stopped tryin' to be a long time ago." He began to struggle back into his long johns. "I'd be obliged if you'd let me get dressed and pull on my boots afore throwing me out into the snow. Unless you plan on putting a bullet 'twixt my eyes which, come to think on it, would be a kindness."

"You skinny, scrawny, sorry jackass! Open your ears, boy. Did I say anything about throwing you out? Shit, Pride, I may be older than you, but there ain't a damn thing wrong with my eyes. I seen that you been toting wood in your britches every now and then. I figured it out right soon after you got here."

"You...knew?" Pride asked. He couldn't have been more floored if one of the wooden wolves had leapt up off the cupboard shelf and bit him, and his face burned with more than the heat from the fire. "You *knew*?"

"Hell yeah, I knew. Figured it didn't matter none." Bear's huge shoulders shrugged. "Your pa thought it mattered though, huh? Sakes alive, for a father to lay his son's back open like that..."

"He took the strop to me, tried to whip it out of me. I think he would've killed me if he'd had the strength to go on any longer than he did. He was bigger than me, but soft. Never lifted nothing heavier than his Bible. He tuckered himself out pretty quick," Pride said. He'd managed to get his arms back into the sleeves of his long johns, but Bear stopped him from pulling it up over his shoulders.

"You was fixin' to take a bath, remember?" he said, giving Pride a little shove. "Go on and finish what you started. Ain't nothing changed. You still reek like the Devil's asshole." Turning, Bear walked off and busied himself in the alcove by his bed, his back to Pride, fussing with something Pride couldn't see. Bless the man, he was trying to give Pride a bit of privacy while he ducked out of his drawers and climbed into the tub.

Bear was a finer man than Pride had ever suspected. Not many would have allowed someone like Pride to stay under their roof. He'd said he'd seen Pride toting a hard-on more than once. Even though Pride had never made a single gesture other than purely friendly ones, Bear must have known what Pride was thinking about to get his pecker up. Knew what thoughts were going through Pride's head when Bear was taking his bath. But he'd never said a word to Pride. Even his own pa would have booted Pride's sinning ass out if it wouldn't have had made Pa look bad to his congregation – unable to save his own son's soul, and all. Not that it had mattered much. Pa had been dead not six months later. Keeled over at the breakfast table, gone on to his reward before he hit the floor.

Pride sighed long and deep as he slipped into the hot water, sinking down and bending his knees until he was submerged up to his chin.

"So what happened to the man?" Bear asked from the other side of the room. "The one your pa caught you with?" Evidently, he wasn't going to let Pride off the hook until he knew the whole story. He suspected that Bear was like a dog with a bone when he wanted a question answered. He'd keep after him until Pride either told him everything or drowned himself in the tub.

"Joe. His name was Joe. He was a hired hand that worked Ol' Man Mullins' spread, down the road a piece from our place. Near 'bout twenty-five years old, I'd say. Me? I was young and stupid, confused as all hell, not sure which end was ass up. He was gentle, sweet. Taught me what to do," Pride answered. "Made me see I wasn't the only one in the world who felt the way I did."

He reached for the soap and the scrub brush and started in on his feet, whisking the stiff bristles across his toes, scraping some of his skin off along with the dirt. "Pa come into the barn one night while we was... well, while we was busy. Lord! His face turned so red I was a-feared his head would explode right off his neck! He was hollering like the Devil himself was roosting in the hay. Somebody must have heard him because men came running to help. Guess they thought Pa was getting murdered from the way he was carrying on."

"What happened?" Bear pressed. Pride looked over and saw that he had forsaken his whittling, and was concentrating on darning a pair of socks that needed mending. Bear was trying to act like their conversation was no more than normal talk between men. Pride would've smiled, if the story hadn't been tearing his heart up all over again.

"The men dragged Joe off while Pa got the strop out. Had my brothers hold me while he whipped me. I guess I must have fainted. I never saw Joe again, but I heard screamin' later that night, after I woke up. Lord, but those screams still haunt me. My brothers told me that the men had smeared honey on Joe's dick and lowered him into the hog pen. Said there wasn't much left of his lower half by the time the hogs were done."

"The hell you say! Lord, that ain't no way for a man to die."

"Yeah, well, it was a long time ago, Bear."

"Still stinks like cow shit on a hot summer day. That water still warm, or do you need more hot?"

"Naw, it's fine, Bear."

"Shit, these socks got more holes than a French whorehouse. Might as well use 'em for rags," Bear grumbled, tossing them back down into the basket. He stood up and stretched. "Best hurry and finish up afore that water gets chilled, Pride. I don't want to have to be nursing you through the ague just 'cause you sat too long in a cold bath."

"Okay, Bear."

"I'm leaving a pair of long johns on the chair for you. They're old ones, but they're clean. Figure you might need to roll up the sleeves and legs a mite, though. I'm heading off to bed. I'm beat." He lit a tallow candle, placing it in a silver holder. Picking it up, he walked into the small alcove, the bed frame creaking as he settled his substantial weight onto it. "Night, Pride."

"Night, Bear," Pride answered, listening as Bear slipped into his bed. "Thank you."

Just like that. Pride's secret was out, and Bear was saying goodnight to him like nothing was different. Still being his same sweet, caring self. Like nothing had changed between them. Damn.

"Pride?"

"Yeah?"

"Just so you know, I think your Pa was wrong. You wasn't hurting nobody that I can see. Hope the bastard's roasting in Hell for what he done to you."

Pride swallowed hard, running the bristles of the scrub brush through his fingers. When he answered, his voice was gruff. "Thanks, Bear."

"Night."

"Night."

The candle was snuffed out, casting the alcove in

shadows. After a while, the only sound in the cabin was swish of the scrub brush bristles over Pride's skin, and Bear's soft snores.

On a bluff high up on the mountain, three men stood looking down at the miles of forested foothills spread out beneath them. Smoke rose in a thin curl from the treetops not fifteen or twenty miles northwest of where they stood.

"There you are, you miserable bastard," Zack whispered. He shielded his eyes with his hand trying to pick out a cabin, but the distance made it impossible.

"Could be somebody's campfire, Zack. How do you know it's a cabin, or that it belongs to this Bear fella we been chasing?" Jeb asked, distractedly. His horse was being ornery this afternoon, sidestepping and dancing on his toes. He pulled at its bridle, clucking under his tongue.

"It's him." Zack's voice was grim, determined. It *had* to be him. Zack wouldn't allow it to be otherwise. Tracked that rat bastard for fifteen fucking years and now only a few short miles separated him from the man who'd killed his daddy and destroyed Zack's life with a single bullet. He lowered his hands to his sides, fisting them into hard, tight balls. "It's him."

Levi eyed the sky and the thick, gray clouds that were beginning to drift in. The temperature had dropped, too. He spat over the edge of the bluff. "Storm comin', Zack. I can smell snow on the wind."

Zack growled, looking up at the sky as if the black look on his face could turn back the storm. "We'll head down, see how far we can get before she breaks. C'mon." He mounted up, his own horse leading his newly stolen one.

They'd just reached the lower foothills when the first fat white flakes began to fall. Within the hour, the wind had picked up to a howl, and the snow was driving in sideways.

"We'd best find someplace to pitch the tent!" Jeb bellowed over the shrieking wind, trotting up closer to Zack to make himself heard. "No telling how bad this is going to get."

"We're going to keep going until I say to stop!" Zack yelled back, turning a threatening look at Jeb. "And that ain't gonna be until we're close enough that he's not going to slip away from me again!"

"But Zack, it's pretty near a blizzard already! It's colder than a witch's tit -- my drawers are near frozen to my skin!" Jeb countered. "And I'm damned hungry! We ain't stopped to eat nothing since breakfast! You're carrying on like catching up with this Bear fella is more important than your own men's lives!"

They were the last complaints Jeb ever made.

The gunshot was muffled by the power of the storm, but there was no easing of the bullet as it plowed into Jeb's forehead, dropping him from his saddle. Smoke rising from the barrel of Zack's gun was whisked away on the wind.

Zack gestured toward Jeb's body with his gun. Levi moved quickly, taking hold of the reins of Jeb's horse, tethering him to his own mount. Jumping down, he relieved Jeb of his gun and what little money he'd had stashed in his pockets. Without exchanging a single word or a backward look, Levi remounted and the two men continued on, leaving Jeb facedown in the snow with blood pooling under his head, the deep dark red stark against the pristine white powder. Within a few minutes the body cooled and snow began to cover it.

Wasn't the first time Zack had been pushed to lose his

temper with a new man. As a matter of fact, Levi was the *only* man Zack could stand to have around for more than a few months at most. Levi knew who was boss, and when to keep his trap shut.

These new boys yammered on worse than old women.

No need to worry about hiding the body. From the corner of Zack's eye he caught a furtive movement in the brush. Something had already been drawn by the smell of blood on the wind. By spring there wouldn't be anything left of Jeb but a few scraps of clothing and an odd bone or two.

They pushed on until they were no more than two or three miles from the area Zack reckoned he'd seen the smoke coming from. Reluctantly, he gave the word to Levi to make camp. Tomorrow. Tomorrow he'd have his revenge.

Chapter Five

A second storm in as many days was howling outside when Bear woke up the next morning. He walked into the main room, smiling down at Pride. He was sleeping on his stomach, nearly lost under the pile of furs and pelts. Looked smaller and younger than ever, more like a boy than a man, with his hair tousled and his face peaceful. Lord knew he'd gone through more Hell than any boy had a right to, though. Only fourteen when his pa had dug ditches into his back with a strop. Damn him.

Bear's meaty hands curled into tight fists. If Pride's pa had been in the room with him, Bear would have pounded him into dust. He was never one to tolerate cruelty, perhaps because of the tragedy in his own life.

Pride must have been up half the night. The cabin was spotless, the dishes cleaned and set back in the cupboard, the skillet scrubbed till it shone. The tub had been emptied, and the buckets placed neatly by the fire. One was full of clean water. Pride must have scooped up a bucket of snow to melt, so they could have coffee in the morning.

Even the sawdust and curls of wood from Bear's whittling had been swept up, and their chairs had been returned to the table. His and Pride's long johns had been washed and wrung out, and hung from the mantle to dry.

No wonder he was still sleeping so soundly. He deserved it, after cleaning up their mess from the night before all by himself. Quiet as a church mouse, too. Bear had never heard him once.

It was a pure pleasure having him stay. Having someone to talk to, someone to share the chores with, eat with, share stories with. Bear was suddenly grateful that another storm had blown up in the night. Pride couldn't leave until it blew itself out and if the snow was too deep, maybe he might see his way clear to stay the winter.

That would be mighty fine, in Bear's book.

Maybe, if Pride stayed, Bear could figure out why he'd had the dream he'd had last night -- the one where Pride had slipped under the patchwork quilt with Bear. The one where they'd both been naked. The one where Pride had kissed him.

Bear passed his hand over the thick, bushy beard that covered most of his face. Never thought to shave, hadn't bothered in years, but the thought suddenly occurred to him that it might be a good idea. He put the thought of the unsettling dream out of his head and bustled off to dig out his straight razor and the leather strop to sharpen it on.

"You shaved!" Pride said, looking twice at Bear. He'd woken up, gone to pee in the bucket after Bear had warned him that it was storming again outside, and had sat down at the table, warming his hands around his cup of morning coffee. All the while he'd been feeling that there was something different, but couldn't put his finger on what it was. His eyes wandered over Bear's face, so different now that the wild forest of black hair wasn't covering it. Pride found that he could barely tear his eyes away.

Bear was a handsome man.

His eyes looked bluer and brighter than they had before, when they'd been reflecting the black of his beard. His nose, the only part of his face other than his forehead that had been completely visible before he'd shaved, seemed stronger, noble somehow. His cheekbones were so high and sharp that Pride wondered if Bear might not have some Indian blood in him. Bear's lips (and he had *two*, something Pride hadn't noticed when Bear's shaggy mustache had covered the upper one), were perfectly shaped, the top one deeply cleft and the bottom sensuously full.

Best not to linger on them, not unless Pride wanted to walk around with an erection again all day.

Pride wondered about Bear's age. He was older than Pride, that was a given, but Pride doubted that even Bear knew his true age. He'd stopped counting the years after he'd moved into the foothills.

Bear's skin was mostly smooth and golden aside from the paler patch along his jaw where his beard had been, still sun-browned from the summer. Laugh lines creased the corners of his eyes, and he had a few worry lines running across his forehead, but he looked no older than thirty-five or so to Pride. His hair, inky black, long and unruly, was without a trace of silver.

"You look good without it, Bear," Pride said softly, not able to stop looking at him. He wanted to memorize that face, carve it into his memory the way Bear carved lines into his whittling, so that Pride would never forget it. Unfortunately, that was doing things to Pride's nether regions that made him squirm uncomfortably in his chair.

"Yeah? I wasn't sure. Been a while since I last shaved," Bear said, his cheeks pinking as he ran his hand across his face. "I...it was itching." Bear stood and moved to the stove, returning with two steaming bowls of oatmeal mush, his mason jar of honey, and a small glass jar of cinnamon. He placed one of the bowls down in front of Pride.

It hadn't itched Bear at all, Pride realized. Pride could tell that Bear had offered him a little white lie about why he'd shaved, as if he had to make an excuse for getting rid of his beard. Pride wondered why Bear felt the need to be less than honest about it, but decided not to say anything. His reasons were his reasons, and none of Pride's business.

"I like it." Pride said, rubbing his own jaw, prickly with several days' worth of stubble. Not that he had much to worry about. His beard was so light and sparse that even several *weeks'* worth of growth would hardly show. "Maybe I should shave my beard. Been a while for me, too."

Bear laughed, showing his straight, white teeth. "You call *that* a beard? Looks like peach fuzz to me."

"Aw, now, there's no cause to go picking on a man's beard, Bear," Pride said, sounding wounded. He couldn't hold on to a straight face, though, and cracked a grin almost immediately. "It ain't much, is it?" he laughed, scratching under his jaw.

"No, it ain't. But you look fine, Pride."

For some reason, that small compliment warmed Pride's belly more than the oatmeal they were eating for breakfast. He hid his smile by spooning another lumpy, white mound into his mouth.

"Listen, Pride... "

"Yeah, Bear?"

"I was thinking... "

"Dangerous habit," Pride chuckled, earning himself a laugh from Bear.

"I was thinking that maybe you should stay the winter."

Pride's hand froze halfway to his mouth, his oatmeal-filled spoon hovering in mid-air. "What?"

"Oh, I know you got plans and all. Got better places to be than holed up in this shack with me, but the weather's got a mind of its own this time of year. Never know when a storm's gonna blow in. The mountains are already next to impossible to cross this late in the season. Snow's deeper up there. There have been times when I've seen it slide down the side of the mountain like a wave of white water, crushing and covering everything in its path. I was just thinking that maybe it would be safer for you bunker down here," Bear said softly, not quite looking Pride in the eye. "Get a start on traveling after the spring thaw."

"You...want me to stay?" Pride asked, wide-eyed.

"Well, yeah, I do. I like you, Pride. I mean, I like your company. Feels like you're a friend."

Pride was stunned. Bear knew what he was, knew what looking at Bear's body did to him. And still, he wanted him to stay. "I don't know what to say, Bear. I'm nothing but a burden to you, eating your food, using up your firewood... "

"I done told you I got plenty put by. I always put up more than I need."

"Then, yes, and thank you kindly, Bear. I don't know how I'll ever repay you for everything you've done for me."

"Don't think on it. You done plenty, yourself – why look at all you done yesterday alone! Helped me with the traps, then helped skin the varmints. Put together supper, and cleaned everything up after, emptied the tub, swept up the mess I made whittling. I would've had to do it all myself, if you weren't here."

"Bear?"

"Yeah?"

"Think maybe you could whittle us up a set of checkers? I'm partial to game, myself," Pride said, feeling his cheeks heat. It was one of the few times in his life that he had no idea of what to say. What do you say to someone who's already saved your life, let you eat at his table, sleep under his roof, and then *asks* you to stay longer?

What do you say to man like that when he makes your blood sing and your groin heat up like water set to simmer on the fire?

Nothing, that's what.

You keep your thoughts inside your head where they belong, and you ask him about checkers.

And when your lips want to flap and tell him everything you've been doing to him in your dreams, you shove a heaping spoonful of piping hot oatmeal mush between them.

He'd gone to work on that checkers set the minute they'd finished breakfast. Pride had gotten all uppity with him when Bear had started to clear his dish from the table. Said that if Bear had cooked, then Pride would clean up, and "*that's just the way of it, Bear.*"

Had a heap of gumption for such a little, skinny varmint. But Bear had handed him his dish without an argument and had settled himself in front of the fire with a fresh stick of wood and his knife. Wouldn't take long at all to whittle the checker pieces. He had a little paint he'd bought last trip into town, thinking he'd try his hand at painting some of his whittlings. Bear figured he could work out a checkerboard with it – maybe paint one right on top of the kitchen table.

It pleased Bear to think of spending the long winter days and nights playing checkers with Pride. Talking. Laughing, maybe.

Pride had found Bear's sourdough starter, and had set himself the task of baking a loaf of bread for their supper. He'd mixed it up early and at the moment he was standing at the table, elbow deep in sticky dough, kneading and pounding the shit out of it.

"I think you done beat that dough to death, Pride," Bear called, looking up from his whittling at an extra-loud bang.

"Nah, I think it's still breathing, Bear," Pride laughed, flipping the whole mess over and commencing to start kneading and pounding again.

"Bread's gonna bake up black and blue if you keep that up."

Pride laughed, and the sound was like music to Bear's ears. He tried to remember the last time he'd laughed so easily with anyone, and realized it had been before his family had been murdered. He felt the emptiness of the years he'd spent alone drain away. Everything around him suddenly seemed brighter, and for the first time Bear found himself looking forward to being cabin-bound all winter.

His thoughts drifted back to the dream he'd had. Bear wasn't a stupid man, and he'd seen a lot in the fifteen years since he'd left home. He knew that men like Pride existed, men who didn't care much for the soft curves of a woman. He'd never had such inclinations himself but since he'd always seen fit to live and let live, Bear just hadn't paid those men much never-mind. Whenever he'd come down off the mountain for supplies, he'd always satisfied his lusts with one or another saloon gal. A few coins and not many more minutes and it was done. The rest of time he'd taken care of the problem himself when it got to be too uncomfortable. For Bear, sex was just another chore a man needed to tend to now and then in order to survive.

But since freeing Pride from that danged tree, it seemed like *men* was all Bear could think about. No, to be honest with himself, that wasn't true. Not *men* – man. One man. Pride.

The dream had been cloudy, foggy. He couldn't even remember the details, only that Pride and him had been naked together in Bear's bed, a-squirming and a-rolling over each other. And Pride had kissed him full on the mouth. That was all he remembered, but damn if that wasn't enough to tent his britches full to bursting every time he thought on it. And even though it made him hard and his body burn with a powerful need, he couldn't stop thinking about it - about Pride.

Sad thing was, even if Pride ripped his 'johns off and danced around in front Bear bare-buck naked, Bear wouldn't have the slightest idea of what to do. Hold him, maybe. Touch him. The thought sent sweet shivers up and down Bear's spine. But Bear knew that even if that happened, he'd never have the nerve to do anything more than stare bug-eyed at Pride. He'd be too afraid of being as gawky as a newborn calf and as clumsy as a full-grown ox. He'd embarrass himself.

Stifling a groan, he shifted in his seat, trying to adjust his pecker with out being obvious about it. Storm or no storm, if this kept up, Bear was going to have to find an excuse to go outside and let the cold undo what he done to himself.

That, or he'd be sporting a wet spot in the front of his britches for all the world and Pride to see. He began to count the minutes until he could go to bed, crawl under his covers, and beat some sense into his dick.

He stood up and stomped over the cupboard, returning to the table with a jug and their two coffee mugs. "Had a powerful thirst just now," he said, his deep voice sounding rough. He poured them both a drink of whiskey, and downed his in one long, burning gulp.

With any luck he'd get Pride dead drunk, and could take care of his problem without having to worry about Pride overhearing him.

Chapter Six

"Pride?"

Bear's deep voice carried over from the alcove. Pride stirred, hearing his name called in his sleep. Groggily, he picked his head up and looked toward Bear's bedroom. "Yeah, Bear?"

Silence stretched so long that Pride began to think that Bear had been talking in his dreams, not that that would surprise him. Bear had drunk enough the night before to put a smaller man into a dead sleep for a week. Hearing nothing, Pride laid his head back down, pushing the furs off. Sleeping this close to the fire kept a man warm enough. He really didn't need any of the furs Bear had insisted he use as bedding.

"Pride...I was wondering... "

"What, Bear? What do you need?"

"Can you teach me, Pride?" Bear asked.

Looking up, Pride saw him standing in the doorway of the alcove, his large frame completely filling it. Dressed only in his long underwear, Pride couldn't help but notice the long, hard bulge of Bear's penis outlined under the grayed wool. Lordy, that man was big *all* over, and that was a fact. Pride felt his balls tighten and his cock harden, and quickly pulled the furs back up to cover his lower half.

"Teach you what, Bear? What are you talking about?" Pride's mouth went dry and he wrenched his eyes away from Bear's groin, trying to see his face in the firelight. He hardly dared believe that Bear was asking him about what Pride thought he was asking about.

"What that man, what was his name? Joe? What he done taught you. Can you teach me?" Bear's voice was a whisper now, edged with a raw need that cut Pride right to the bone. "What men do together."

"Bear... do you know what you're asking?" If Pride hadn't already been lying on the floor, Bear's request would have dropped him face first onto the pine planks.

"Yeah, I do. I been having dreams, Pride, dreams about you, last night and tonight. You were doing things to me that..." Bear said, trailing off. He looked so uncomfortable standing there, wringing his big, beefy hands. Pride could tell even without the benefit of strong light that Bear was blushing a deep rosy red. "It's been so long since I... "

"You ever had a man touch you, Bear?" Pride asked softly, sitting up. He patted the furs next to him, encouraging Bear to sit down.

Hesitantly, not looking Pride in the eyes, Bear lowered his bulk to the floor. "No, never. Never thought about it, neither. But lately, seems like that's all I *can* think about. I know what to do with women, but how do two men... I mean, how do you... "

Pride smiled, looking up at Bear. "I think about you all the time Bear. You said that you knew that, knew it from the first. 'Course, I never would've brought it up, never would have asked you about it. If you really want me to show you, then you don't need to ask me twice. But I have to know that it's what you want, that you know what's going to happen between us."

"That's just it! I *don't* know what's going to happen."

"What did we do in your dreams, Bear?" Pride asked gently.

Bear ran a large hand through his tangle of thick black hair. "I don't remember much. You kissed me. And I held you. Tight. Close. Am I wrong for wanting this, Pride?"

"No, you ain't wrong. You're just lonely is all, Bear."

"No, it ain't that. I been lonely a long time, since the night my family was murdered. This is different. You're my friend, Pride. But I want more. I just don't know what it is that I'm hankering after. Teach me, Pride."

Bear's words brought the burn of tears to the back of Pride's throat. "I know what you're saying. You're my friend, too. Feels like you're the only true friend I've had in a long, long time. Look at me, Bear," he whispered, reaching up and gently cupping Bear's chin with his fingers. He could feel the rough whiskers that were already starting to grow back in along Bear's jaw. A bolt of heat seared Pride's groin as he wondered what those scratchy hairs would feel like scraping over his skin. "I don't want to do anything that's gonna hurt our friendship."

"It won't, Pride. I just want…I need…" Bear trailed off, not able to find the words to express the desire that Pride saw burning in his eyes.

Raising himself up to his knees, Pride leaned in and kissed Bear softly, without any pressure or demands, just a light brushing of his lips against Bear's mouth. "Ah, Bear," he sighed, "you taste just like I knew you would. Like honey and coffee and whiskey. Lay back, Bear. I want to kiss you a mite more."

Bear's deep blue eyes looked black in the firelight, wide with wonder and more than a little nervousness, but he did as Pride asked. Pride shivered, knowing that what he'd wanted since he first laid eyes on Bear was being offered to him, part and parcel. All of Bear, wherever

Pride wanted to touch him, taste him. He took a deep breath, steadying himself. Got to go slow now. Easy.

The neck of Bear's long johns exposed a deep vee of his chest. Black hair curled over his smooth skin, and Pride slid his hand across it, feeling the silken texture of is under his palm. He slipped his hand under the fabric of Bear's underwear, coming to rest over one of his nipples. Rubbing the tiny nub under his palm until it tightened, he worried it between his fingers. Leaning over Bear, Pride kissed him again, longer this time, harder. He swept his tongue over Bear's lower lip, gently pushing it between them until Bear opened for him.

Sweet and tangy and hot, that was the taste of Bear, Pride decided.

Bear's groan shot a fevered spike though Pride's balls, and his cock hardened to steel. As Bear began to hesitantly return his kisses, each one growing longer and more heated, deeper, Pride rolled his hips forward a bit, digging his prick into Bear's thigh.

"Lordy, Pride! Is that your… "

"Yeah. Feel it? That's what you done to me, Bear. Made me hard for you. I want to touch you now, Bear. Touch your cock. You okay with that?" Pride asked softly, kissing the corners of Bear's mouth, his cheeks, and his eyelids. Sweet man. Sweet, sweet man.

Bear moaned, his body instinctively turning toward Pride. He nodded, his thick fingers touching Pride's face timidly, as if he weren't certain he had the right. Pride turned his head and kissed Bear's palm.

Lightly, he ran his fingers over the hard shaft of Bear's cock, feeling his heat rise through the fabric of his underwear. He was big and thick, as hot as the fire in the hearth and as hard as the stone used to build it. Sweet Christ on the Cross, Pride wanted nothing more than to rip open those threadbare long johns and take proper hold of it, taste it and lick it until Bear squirmed under his hand and mouth. His hand stroked its length, squeezing it lightly through the wool of Bear's long johns.

"Oh, *oh God*, Pride!" Bear suddenly growled. Pride felt Bear's belly tighten, his cock jerking under his hand, the strong scent of man and sex filling the air as wetness soaked Bear's underwear.

"Bear!" Pride moaned, rubbing himself against Bear's muscular thigh. Feeling Bear's seed hot and wet under his hand pushed Pride over the edge without warning. He came in his long johns, seeing stars and shuddering hard.

Too quick, as fast as his first time, rubbing against Joe in the dark shadows of the barn. But sweeter too, because there was no hiding, no need for secrecy. No fear of pain or being caught. Just sweet pleasure, and happiness in knowing he'd given something back to the man who'd saved his life and given him shelter.

"I'm sorry, Pride," Bear whispered, his body stiffening as he looked down between them.

"Don't be. Lord knows I wasn't no better. Been too long for either of us, I reckon. Next time will be better, Bear. Longer. Sweeter."

"Next time?"

Pride picked his head up from where he'd laid it on Bear's massive chest, listening to his heart thudding under his ear. "You...don't you want there to *be* a next time, Bear?" Pride felt his belly clench. Maybe Bear had just wanted a one shot deal at this. Pride wanted much, much more than that – a winter's worth, a lifetime, maybe.

"You wouldn't mind?"

"Bear, I got to tell you something. I never, ever would have said this to you before, but I need you to know this now. I've had my fill of grinding and rubbing in the dark, one man or another wanting a quick fuck while we was out riding fence or herding cattle. They never meant nothing to me. I never meant nothing to them either, I reckon.

"But you and me, we're different. What we got is different, Bear. Only knew you a couple three days, but already my stomach gets tied up in knots whenever I think about leaving."

Bear was silent for a minute, a long minute that seemed to stretch and stretch for Pride. He bit the inside of his cheek, his nerves fraying more and more as that long-drawn-out minute went on. *Say something, Bear. I want you, Pride. I hate you, Pride. Fuck you, Pride, you dimwitted jackass. Anything, Bear, just please, for the love of all that's holy, say* something.

"Good."

"Pardon?"

"Good. Good that you'll be staying," Bear said finally, his voice gruff. He cleared his throat then sat up, looking down at Pride. "I think I got some feelings for you, too, Pride. I just ain't sorted them out yet. You're my friend, but...maybe you might be more than that, too. Maybe not. I just don't know."

"I understand, Bear," Pride said, smiling. "Well, we both got some cleaning up to do," he continued, picking at the sticky wet patch at the crotch of his long johns. "How about I heat us up some water and we get washed up?"

Bear nodded, looking embarrassed. "Yeah. Any of that sourdough left? I'm powerful hungry all of a sudden like. Bread and honey would slide down real easy 'bout now."

Pride laughed. "I swear, Bear, you must've been born with a hollow leg. I ain't never seen a man that could put away more vittles than you, and not have a single ounce go to fat."

"I always had a big appetite. My Pa and brothers did,

too. We was all big. Used to eat so much that my Ma would threaten to put a trough in the kitchen 'stead of a table."

Pride laughed. "Yeah, we still got half a loaf left over from supper. How about I fry us up some bacon to go with it?"

"Sounds good. Pride?"

"Yes, Bear?"

"How long you think it'll be until we can have that *next time* you was talking about?"

Pride laughed, leaned up to kiss Bear on his scruffy jaw, and then set about putting water on the fire to warm.

Chapter Seven

Bear had washed out their long johns and hung them near the fire to dry, and they'd both gone to bed naked.

No more sleeping on the floor in front of the fire for Pride. Bear had insisted that he share Bear's bed. After all, they weren't exactly strangers anymore, and there didn't seem any reason to keep a distance from one another. It was a large bed, wide and deep, and stuffed high with goose feathers. Still, with Bear being as big as he was, Pride had spent most of the night spooned up next to him, Bear's hot flesh pressing against his backside.

That *next time* had come quicker either of them had anticipated -- 'round about in the middle of night, to be exact. Bear's hard length nestled snug against his ass and the rest of Bear's warm body curled around Pride had sparked all kinds of decadent dreams. Pride's cock had woken him out of a dead sleep, fully erect and leaking with need. All Pride had had to do was roll over and he found himself locked in Bear's arms, his soft lips hungrily devouring his own.

Bear wasn't even fully awake. His eyes were half-lidded, sleepy and moony. Pride smiled against his lips, knowing that Bear was still dreaming and that, judging from the length of steel that was poking him in the belly and the fingers that reached around to cup his ass, he was dreaming of Pride and what they'd done together. Were *doing* together.

The second time wasn't any slower than the first. Seems they were both too hard for one another, even with Bear still half-asleep. For his part, it was the knowing that he and Bear could sleep in the same bed and make love whenever and wherever they wanted that had Pride's shotgun cocked and fired in record time. It was the *freedom* of it that got him up and over the edge.

A few minutes of gentle rubbing, foreskin to foreskin, and it was over again. Bear resumed snoring almost without even realizing that he'd come, and totally unconcerned with the mess. Pride chuckled, cleaned them off as best he could with a corner of the quilt then snuggled back down into Bear's arms to pass the remainder of the night.

It was mid-morning by the time they woke up, both taking a care not to look at the other while they dressed, like newlyweds too shy to admit that they'd been sliding skin-to-skin the night before. Both nursed a headache from the whiskey they'd drunk, and Bear found himself nursing a sudden case of guilt as well as a hang-over.

"Coffee will be ready in short order," Bear said, setting the pot to boil on the stovetop. He looked over at Pride, who was peeking out the front door. "Has it stopped snowing yet? How deep is it?"

"'Bout another foot, I'd say," Pride answered, closing the door. "She's all blue skies and sunshine, for now anyway."

"Good. Got more traps I wanna check today. Want to come along? Might be the last time we can get out until spring."

"Might as well. Think we should cut more firewood while we're at it?"

"Couldn't hurt none."

They fell silent as Pride shuffled to the table and sat down. He folded his hands on the table, staring down at his calloused knuckles, while Bear looked everywhere but at Pride.

Both of them seemed fixed on not mentioning the night before. Even though they were talking, it was as though there was an invisible wall between them, and it was making Bear uncomfortable.

"Bear, I should've told you last night that you were wonder..."

Bear's back stiffened, his attention suddenly riveted by the coffee pot. "Don't say it, Pride. I can't think on what we done in broad daylight."

Bear's growl cut Pride's words off as if he'd slapped him in the face. Moments ticked by until he spoke again. "You're sorry we done it." Pride's voice was soft, thick with hurt, and edged with anger.

"I didn't say that! Don't be putting words into my mouth, Pride." Bear banged the skillet down onto the cast iron stove with a loud *clang*.

Silence filled the room, the tension growing so thick between them that Bear felt the weight of it pressing down on his shoulders, making it difficult to breathe. It was too much. Everything he'd been feeling for the past couple of days, the need and the want, the happiness, had clashed headfirst with the guilt that had been simmering in his gut since he'd awoken that morning. It was one thing to *know* about other men doing things like this, but Bear was finding out that it was another to jump in with both feet and roll around in it. He'd never even *thought* about another man's body before, or having a man touch his. Now it seemed that it was all he *did* think about.

"Goddamn it, Pride! What did you do to me?" He spun around, his fists balled up at his sides, his face pale.

Pride sprang to his feet, glaring at Bear. "*Me*? I warned you, Bear! I asked you if you was sure! Told you it was gonna change everything." He pointed an accusing finger at Bear. "You said you didn't care. Said you wanted it. Wanted *me*."

"I know I did!" Bear yelled, his face flushing. "That's what's got my gut so twisted up!"

"So you lied? For what, Bear? So you could use me for a quick fuck? Well, that's fine. Ain't no harm done," Pride yelled, the bitterness in his voice cutting through to Bear's heart. "After all, you saved my life. Seems the least I could do, but you could've just told me that was all you wanted. Didn't have to lie about being friends, about maybe being more than friends." Pride's eyes welled up even as his fist struck the tabletop, rattling their coffee cups and plates. "I'll be gone as soon as I can pull on my boots."

Bear roared, charging across the room. He caught Pride by the shoulders, pushing him roughly against the wall. "I didn't lie! I *never* lie! I *did* want you! I still do! I just don't know *why*," he thundered, his hands fisting in the wool of Pride's long johns. He slammed Pride against the wall. "Goddamn it, Pride! Don't you fucking say that again. Don't you say that you're leaving me!" His own eyes went wide with sudden desperation. "You can't leave now. Not *now*!"

Leaning down, he smashed his mouth against Pride's, his big body crushing Pride's back against the wall. He threaded his fingers into Pride's pale hair, his rough palms cupping his bristled cheeks. Breaking away, he leaned his forehead against Pride's, breathing heavily. "I just need to work things out in my head. Need to figure out what I want."

"You can't have it both ways, Bear. Can't touch me at night and then hate me for it in the morning," Pride whispered.

"I don't hate you. Don't go, Pride."

"I can't stay. I don't want to see disgust in your eyes when you look at me, knowing the only time you'll touch me is in the dark, after you've had a slug or two from your jug."

"I'm touching you now."

"Yeah, but is it because you want to, or because you don't want to be left alone?"

Bear didn't answer. He squeezed his eyes shut, holding his breath, hoping that Pride wouldn't see the confusion he was feeling.

"That's what I figured. You don't make a home with somebody just so that you can have someone else's snores to listen to at night. A warm body you can rub up against in the middle of the night, then pretend like nothing's happened come morning."

"That ain't how I feel."

"I know, Bear. Trouble is, you don't know *what* you feel. And that's okay, really. It's just that I can't sleep in your bed while you try to make up your mind. I got to leave."

"You don't have to leave! Goddamn it, Pride... "

"I'm sorry, Bear. But if I stay, I'll only get hurt worse. I've been hurt enough."

"Fine, then! Leave!" Bear yelled, giving Pride a push that rattled him against the wall. "Go on, get! Don't need you anyhow. Done fine on my own before I met your sorry ass, and I'll do just as fine after you're gone." Anger and crushing disappointment flooded him, making him see red. He turned on his heel, pulled on his pants, shirt, boots, and bearskin cloak, and blew out of the cabin like a force of nature.

Pride stared at the closed door for a long time, swallowing hard and shaking. Damn it. He should've known better. Should have known not to let himself give Bear more than a passing *how-do*. Should've left that very first day. Before he'd grown to like Bear. Before he'd tasted how sweet Bear's lips were, how gentle his big hands could be. Before he'd let himself come to *care*.

Now he was worse off than he'd been before he'd gotten to Bear's cabin. He wished to God that he were still trussed up to that tree. Shit, he wished that damned cougar was picking him out of its teeth right now.

Tears stung his eyes as he gathered up his clothes and slowly got dressed. He'd been on his own since he was fourteen. He'd lived with loneliness every day of his sorry life, and over time it had eased into a dull ache that had grown so familiar that it became just another part of living, a pain that seemed so normal, he hardly even noticed it anymore. But having someone – even if it was only for a couple of days – changed a man. Make him remember how much it hurt to be alone.

Right now that pain was white-hot, searing Pride to the bone.

Damn it! He only had himself to blame. He'd allowed himself all kinds of nice dreams, sweet ones where he and Bear would spend the summers hunting and fishing, and the long winters holed up in his cabin, whittling and playing checkers, and making love. Pipe dreams. Impossible dreams.

Well, it was over now. Bear had told him to get gone, and Pride was never one to stay where he wasn't wanted. He slid his arms into the sleeves of the elk skin coat, hating having to take even that much from Bear. But without the coat he wouldn't make it an hour hiking up into the snow-covered, bitterly cold mountains.

Then again, maybe he shouldn't even try to make it over the pass. Maybe he should just give up. Lie down in the soft powder and let it end once and for all.

Not that it mattered much anyway. With no supplies and no weapons, he was as good as dead. He'd never make it over the mountains, and he wouldn't make it down to St. Elmo's, either. All he could do was to make damn sure that he got far enough away so that Bear wouldn't find him later, frozen blue and probably gnawed at. No matter how much Bear had hurt him and pissed him off, Pride wouldn't do that to him.

He damned himself again for caring.

Opening the door, he stepped outside into the bitter wind. Taking one last look at the inside of Bear's cozy cabin, remembering Bear sitting by the fire whittling; remembering the scent of Bear's skin and the feel of his body spooned up next to his, Pride closed the door and started walking.

Bear's footprints headed in the same direction Pride needed to go, up through the foothills toward the mountains. He followed them, keeping his eyes peeled for Bear's big body in the distance. Pride figured he'd skirt into the brush if he saw him. He told himself that the last thing he wanted was to meet up with Bear. He didn't want to have to say goodbye again, and it would kill him pure and simple if Bear looked at him with hate in his eyes.

He should have gone another way, taken a different route through the thick trees. But a small part of him, a part he wouldn't acknowledge, *wanted* another glimpse of Bear, another memory to store away, even if it was a painful one. He didn't want his last memory to be Bear glaring at him, snarling with anger.

The air was clear, the snow on the ground making everything seem even more quiet than usual. The only sound was the crunch of Pride's boots in the snow. The going was slow and hard, tramping through two feet of fresh powder, and Pride's skin broke out into a sweat under his heavy elk hide coat. But unlike his body, his feet were another story. He hadn't walked far through the deep snow before they felt frozen solid in his boots, numb and aching at the same time, and the skin of his face was whipped raw by the freezing gusts that buffeted him. He hunched over into wind, pressing on.

Suddenly, a loud *crack* sounded, shattering the silence, and drawing Pride's mind from the misery in his feet and his heart. It echoed all around, bouncing off the rocks and trees of the hills. Pride spun in one direction then the other, trying to figure out where it had come from. No one else lived within miles of Bear's cabin. Couldn't be that anyone was up here hunting with two feet of snow on the ground. Could be that Bear shot a deer.

A small, nagging fear told Pride otherwise.

"Nothing goes to waste in my house." Bear had said that not a few days ago, right after he'd told Pride that he had more than enough food put away for the winter. He wouldn't shoot an animal if he didn't need the meat. Bear wasn't the kind of man who enjoyed killing for sport.

Maybe he'd stumbled on a pack of timber wolves.

Pride's stomach fell to his feet as he was hit with a sudden mental image of Bear backed against a tree, a pack of snarling wolves snapping at him, feinting in and out, ready to tear him apart.

Before he even knew that he was moving, Pride's feet were carrying him over the snow, his knees lifting high, following Bear's tracks as fast as he could.

Chapter Eight

Cresting a small rise, Pride spotted a large dark shape lying flat against the white ground in the distance, as still as a stone.

He'd recognize that bearskin cloak anywhere.

Pride pushed himself to move even faster through the deep snow, his heart pounding as his panic grew. As he neared Bear, his sharp eyes caught a movement higher up on the side of the hill, something large crashing through the brush. Whatever it was, it was making a beeline for Bear, and Pride aimed to get to him first.

Another shot rang out, and Pride felt a bullet whistle by perilously close to his head, so close that the damn thing might have parted his hair. It hadn't been Bear that had fired his gun at all. It was someone else.

Heaving his body forward, his legs straining and his breath ragged, Pride pushed himself forward the last few feet until he reached Bear. He dropped to his knees next to him, hunkering low to make himself a smaller target.

Sprawled out on his stomach, a pool of bright red was seeping into the snow under Bear's right shoulder.

"Oh God, Bear," Pride whispered, afraid to turn him over, afraid he'd see dead, glazed eyes staring up at him.

A slight moan gave him hope, and he turned Bear over onto his back as gently as he could.

"Damn, Pride... I'm sorry about what I said. You didn't have to shoot me," Bear whispered, touching his wounded shoulder. A small hole had been opened in the heavy bearskin, and his fingers came away red.

"I didn't shoot you, you old fool!" Pride answered, gently touching Bear's face. "I was behind you the whole time, and on my worst day I never shot a man in the back." Bear *had* been shot though, that was plain. And whoever done it was trampling down through the brush, getting closer every minute. Another gunshot split the air, kicking up a bit of snow just inches from where Pride was kneeling.

Pride's face hardened with an expression he hadn't worn since the War. Stony. Determined. Merciless. He snatched up Bear's shotgun from where it had fallen in the snow when Bear had been shot, and cocked it. One shell, one shot. Well, he'd make damn sure he'd make the fucker count. Narrowing his eyes, he took careful aim at the movement in the trees above them, and pulled the trigger. The thunder of the shotgun seemed to roll on forever across the hills.

A scream rent the air, shrill and undulating. A moment later, Pride threw himself down on top of Bear as the unseen enemy returned his fire. Digging in Bear's pockets for his spare shells, he reloaded and took aim again, firing both barrels into the same area of trees.

Another voice rose up to join the scream, shrieking and cursing, but then the movement stilled and after a few moments quiet returned.

"C'mon, Bear. You got to get up now. We can't stay here, out in the open. I don't know how many of them there are, or how badly I shot them. Could be I just winged them. We got to get back to the cabin afore they come after us again," Pride whispered, helping Bear sit up. Bear's grunt of pain made Pride wince with sympathy, but he couldn't let him rest. Not now. Not with God only knew how many men in the trees hunting for them.

He took only enough time to reload the shotgun before helping heave Bear's bulk up out of the snow.

Pride thanked his lucky stars that Bear was a strong man, even wounded. He tucked himself up under Bear's good shoulder and took on a good deal of Bear's weight as they struggled through the deep snow, but he never would have been able to carry him.

No other shots rained down on them, but that didn't mean that the men who'd fired on them had given up. But since the siege had ended – at least temporarily -- Pride realized that there couldn't have been more than a couple of them, and that if there were two then he must have at least wounded both of them since he and Bear hadn't been fired upon again. Still, he cringed with every step, expecting to hear the blast of a rifle from behind them.

Between his worry over Bear's injury and his fear that they'd both be shot in the back before they could make it back, the cabin seemed a million miles away to Pride. He breathed a sigh of relief when the dovetailed logs and stovepipe chimney came into view, but didn't allow himself to believe that they'd reached the cabin alive until he kicked open the front door and helped Bear inside.

Pride walked Bear to his bed, easing off his bearskin cloak. He grabbed a folded, spare blanket from on top of Bear's chest of drawers, and pressed it against Bear's wound. "Hold this here, tight now, Bear. Got to get the bleeding to stop. I need to take a look see out the window."

"Don't get your fool head shot off, okay?" Bear said in a hoarse voice, wincing as he pressed the shirt to his bloodied shoulder.

"I'll try my best," Pride answered, finding a small smile for him. "As long as you don't go bleeding to death on me, okay?"

"Deal."

Pride raced back, latching the door and manhandling the heavy cupboard over to block it. He next went to the window, pulling back the small piece of hide that covered it and eased open the shutters a crack.

He could see nothing, just the mounds of snow marred only by his and Bear's footprints, and the thick darkness of the forested hills. Pulling the shutters closed and latching them, he dropped the drape. Resting the shotgun against the wall under the window, he trotted back into the alcove to check on Bear.

Carefully, Pride unbuttoned and peeled back Bear's shirt and underwear. Using the blanket, Pride cleaned away some of the blood that had coated Bear's shoulder and chest. The bullet had pierced a small hole, burned black around the edges, into the fleshy part of Bear's right shoulder, just under the joint. Gently slipping his fingers around to Bear's back, he felt for an exit wound, but found none. The bullet was lodged somewhere in Bear's shoulder.

Luckily, the bleeding had slowed to a trickle, but Pride worried about how much blood Bear had already lost. Plus, he knew all too well what could happen to a man who'd been shot and left unattended. He'd known many men to survive a battle only to die in the days and weeks afterward when infection had turned their wounds gangrenous.

"How're you holding up, Bear?" he asked, easing Bear's shirt off. He did the same with Bear's long johns, leaving him naked from the waist up. He gently pressed the bloodied blanket back to the wound.

"Ouch! I was feeling better afore you came in and

started picking at it," Bear grumbled. His face was pale and strained, his brow creased with pain.

Pride chuckled softly. "Gonna feel worse before you feel better, I reckon. And you're gonna hate me more than shit pie before I'm done with you." He took a deep breath and looked into Bear's eyes. "Gotta take it out, Bear," he said, gently but firmly.

"No, you don't. You can just leave it be, Pride."

"Sorry, Bear. It has to come out, or it'll get infected."

Bear growled, frowning at Pride. "No, it won't. I'm fine."

"I hate to be the one to tell you this, Bear, but you got a hole in your hide. You ain't fine."

"You see anybody out there?"

"Would I be back here jawing with you if I did? No, I didn't see nobody, and don't change the subject. I'm going to go heat up some water, and get that jug of whiskey out. Where'd you stick that Bowie knife of yours?"

Bear paled even more, shaking his head. "Oh shit, Pride... "

"It'll be okay, Bear. Promise," Pride said, cupping Bear's chin with his hand, forcing Bear to look him in the eye. "I need to do this. I wouldn't hurt you if I didn't have to, but if we leave it in there it could kill you. Ain't gonna let that happen, no way, no how." Forgetting their argument, forgetting that Bear had all but thrown him out, Pride leaned down and kissed Bear softly. "Ain't gonna lose you, Bear."

Bear swallowed hard, then nodded. "All right, Pride. You do it. But if I scream like a little girl, I'm hoping you won't hold it against me."

Pride chuckled. "Gonna hold it over your head every day for the rest of your life."

"I hate you already."

Laughing, glad that Bear still had a sense of humor, he

got up and kindled a small fire in the hearth, setting a pot of water over it to boil. He stole another glance out of the window, but saw nothing. Could be that whoever it was that had shot at them had retreated into the hills to nurse their own wounds.

At least, that was what he hoped and prayed. 'Course what Pride truly wished was that his shots had been dead-on and had ended up drilling holes right between the bastards' beady eyes. If not, they could be fixing to fire on the cabin at any moment. Pushing the worry of being attacked aside, he concentrated on Bear.

The jug was where Bear had left it, on the top shelf of the cupboard. Pride was grateful that he hadn't managed to knock it off and break it when he'd moved the wooden cabinet over to block the door. Carrying it into the alcove, he sat down on the bed, uncorking it and lifting it to Bear's lips. The strong smell of whiskey mixed with the odors of sweat and blood that hung in the air.

"Take a good long swallow, Bear. As a matter of fact, take a few. Better if you was passed out drunk when I do this."

Bear nodded, taking a drink. He coughed, and groaned at the pain the movement caused his shoulder. "Damn, feels like a fucking cannonball went through me."

Pride laughed. "Trust me. If it was a cannonball that hit you I'd be worrying about finding all your pieces, not taking out a little bitty piece of lead."

"Thanks. That makes me feel *so* much better, Pride," Bear grumbled, frowning at Pride over the mouth of the jug.

"My pleasure. Who the hell are they, Bear? Who'd want to shoot you down?"

"Don't know. Don't have any enemies that I know about. Only acquainted with a handful of people down in St. Elmo's, and I don't know *them* all that good. I only make two or three trips down there a year for supplies."

"Well, somebody's sure enough got a hard-on for you. Good thing he was a poor shot, else I'd be fixing to dig your grave instead of a bullet out of your shoulder."

Bear cringed again, and took another long swallow of whiskey.

Pride continued to sit on the edge of the bed, urging Bear to drink the belly-burning booze until Bear's head began to loll on his neck. Putting the jug down, he helped Bear lay down. Fishing Bear's Bowie knife out from his thigh sheath, he returned to the hearth where the pot of water was boiling.

He held the blade in the fire until it began to glow red, then carried it and the pot of water into the alcove, placing them on the nightstand near the bed. He dug through Bear's chest of drawers until he found a clean shirt, a faded, red-checked flannel that had seen better days, and tore it into wide strips.

Bear's eyes were closed and he was snoring lightly, his head turned to the side. Pride sat on the edge of the mattress, stiffened his spine and grit his teeth, then poured a goodly amount of whiskey directly over the wound.

Even in his sleep, the burning of the alcohol on the open wound roused Bear. He shrieked and bolted halfway up, blinking his eyes open and staring accusingly at Pride.

"Sorry, Bear. Had to."

"Fuck'n baz..." Bear's growl was slurred, and even as he spoke he laid back down on the mattress, his eyes rolling up into his head. Pride waited until he'd slumped back into a faint before picking up one of the bandages he'd made out of Bear's clean shirt and dipping it into the hot water. Using it to wash down Bear's shoulder and chest, he cleaned the blood from the wound.

Sending a prayer to Heaven and hoping that God was still turning his ear toward a sinner like himself, Pride took the knife to Bear's shoulder. Carefully, he slid the blade into Bear's flesh, reopening and slightly widening the wound. Digging around, wincing every time Bear moaned as the pain dragged him back toward consciousness, Pride used the blade of the Bowie to feel for the bullet. He breathed a sigh of relief when he felt the blade hit something hard. Working slowly, he eased the bullet up and out of Bear's shoulder, grabbing it with his fingers. Dousing the wound with alcohol again, he wiped the fresh blood from Bear's skin.

Tearing the rest of Bear's clean shirt into strips, he bandaged the wound, which was bleeding freely again, wrapping the strips over his shoulder and under his arm, and tying them in back. He sat for a long while with his hand pressed against the bandages, until the bleeding had slowed again and Bear rested more quietly, his other hand gently stroking Bear's hair.

Lord, he had come so close to losing Bear that his gut twisted to think on it. Pride's hand was shaking when he picked up the blood-soaked shirt Bear had been wearing and stared at the hole in it for a few moments. A few inches to the left and the bullet might have hit Bear's head or his chest. Goddamn fucking bastards. They'd almost killed him. He angrily tossed the shirt into a corner of the room, along with the bloody blanket.

After placing the small, blood-coated, misshapen lump of pewter-colored lead on top of Bear's nightstand, Pride carefully undressed Bear. He removed his boots and pants, and pulled his long johns off the rest of the way. Picking up the edge of the patchwork quilt, he covered Bear to his chin. Sitting on the edge of the bed, he watched Bear sleep for a long time, his breathing deep and even.

He'd done all he could. With a little bit of luck and a lot of care, the wound might heal clean. He prayed that Bear wouldn't develop a fever. If he did, chances were good that Pride would lose him after all, and the thought near froze his breath in his chest.

Fighting the exhaustion that threatened to drop him like a stone, he Pride searched Bear's pockets for extra shells, then walked into the main room. Piling the ammunition on the kitchen table, he picked up the shotgun, cradling it in his arms, then sat down and prepared to stand watch throughout the night.

Levi had been gutshot by the first round, and although the second bullet that the smaller man had fired had missed them, the third had grazed Zack's right arm. He'd recognized the bastard, too. Goddamn if it wasn't the same fella they'd come across in the woods a few days before. How the hell he'd come to be with Bear was beyond Zack's reckoning. Should've put a bullet in his head when Zack had had the chance, instead of leaving him tied to that tree. Well, he'd never make *that* mistake again.

The pain in his arm burned like hellfire, and Zack had never been a passable shot with his left hand. His only option had been to turn tail and melt back into the hills, even though he ached to go after the two bastards and finish what he'd started.

The horses had scattered when the shooting had begun. Now Zack was half-carrying, half-dragging Levi back up the hills to where they'd made camp during the storm. If it weren't for the fact that Levi had been with him for the past decade and a half, Zack would've just left him behind. He wasn't going to last the night anyhow. But Zack figured he owed him that much.

Laying Levi down in the snow outside of the hide tent they'd pitched, Zack kindled a fire and stripped out of his coat and shirt. Damn bullet had cut a furrow through the skin of his forearm that was near a half-inch deep, and bleeding like a sumbitch. Shivering, he dug into his coat pocket with his good hand, pulling out a large, dirty, gray handkerchief. Tying it around his arm, he used his teeth to help knot it in place, before pulling his shirt and coat back on. "Goddamn bastard. Gonna kill him for sure, gut him like a fish if I can get close enough. Make him suffer long and hard, make him wish he was dead," he promised himself.

Levi moaned, his hands clenched over his belly wound, blood flowing through his fingers, and Zack began to regret that he hadn't left him behind. Damn, if he kept on like that Zack might have to waste a bullet on him, and his ammunition was already on the low side. But he sure as shit wasn't going to spend the night listening to those bubbling, gurgling groans.

Be best if Levi just up and died and got it over with.

Zack stood up and went after the horses. He found two, one more than he was going to need, and called it a day. Back at the campsite, Levi's face had gone gray, and his eyes were closed. He was still breathing and bleeding, but at least he'd stopped that godawful moaning.

Rooting around in his saddlebag, Zack fished out a can of beans and opened them, heating them up over the fire. Sitting and staring at the flames, he ate the barely-warmed beans with his fingers and drank whiskey out of his hipflask, the hate in his gut souring the taste in his mouth.

All Zack could think of was killing Bear and how he was going to make the interfering little bastard that was with him suffer for costing Zack his right-hand man and his chance at revenge. The map wasn't even important anymore – then again, it never had been, really. That was only an excuse he'd given Jeb and Levi to keep their traps shut over his plan to head up into the mountains now and not wait until spring. The only thing that had ever counted to Zack was revenge. The treasure was just icing on the cake.

Swearing, he threw the empty can into the trees. As much as Zack hated to admit it, his vengeance was going to have to wait until after the spring thaw. He was hurting, low on ammunition and supplies, and it was getting colder by the minute. If he got caught out in the open by another storm, he wasn't sure he'd survive.

Glancing over at Levi, Zack frowned at the moans he was making again. Levi always had been a half-step slow and quarter-foot behind, and the way he was setting about dying didn't seem to be no different than the way he'd done everything else in his life. He was taking his sweet ass time about it, and Zack wasn't keen on letting darkness fall while he had a half-dead man dripping blood all over his campsite. That'd draw wolves quicker than shit drew flies.

Shaking his head, Zack walked over and hunkered down next to Levi. Ignoring the pain in his arm, he grabbed hold of Levi's feet and dragged him through the snow as far from his campsite as he could. Pulling out his pocketknife, he slit Levi's throat from ear to ear, jumping back to avoid most of the resulting spray of blood. By the time Zack had wiped his blade clean on Levi's shirt and stood up, Levi was finally stone cold dead. He took Levi's guns and money purse then pulled off Levi's boots almost as an afterthought. No sense in letting them go to waste – Levi had bought them brand new just a few months prior, and they were hardly broke in.

Without another thought to the man who'd spent fifteen years at his side, Zack left him for the vultures and returned to his camp, kicking snow over the trail of blood Levi had left in his wake.

Next spring. At the first thaw, Zack would be back

with plenty of guns and ammunition, and for Bear and his new friend there would be hell to pay.

Zack would see to it. He'd sworn it on his daddy's grave. And now, after the bastards had shot him, it was personal.

Chapter Nine

Bear was proving to be a very poor patient.

That morning Pride had been tempted to whack him upside the head with the cast iron skillet, just to put an end to his grumbling for a time.

"You done cleaned the damn thing yesterday, Pride! There ain't no call to have to do it again today. I ain't done nothing to get it dirty. Shit, how could I? You barely let me out of bed!"

"For the last time, Bear, it ain't *dirt* I'm worried about. It's infection. You're sweating, ain't you? Gotta keep it clean, or it'll fester."

"Fester my ass! You just like to torture me."

"Yeah, that's it. I *live* to play nursemaid to you."

"Nobody's keeping you here," Bear grumbled. But his good hand had shot out and grabbed hold of Pride's, squeezing it lightly, and his eyes told him that he didn't mean what he'd said.

Pride knew it wasn't the pain that was making Bear surly – it was the helplessness he felt. Bear was a strong man, used to fending for himself, and hadn't taken kindly to Pride ordering him to stay put while Pride took care of him.

Could be that Pride was going overboard, keeping Bear to his bed most of the time, not letting him lift a finger to do anything but feed himself. But he couldn't help it. He wasn't taking a single chance that anything could go wrong with the healing process. Bear's wound had scabbed over nicely, hadn't swelled up or started leaking pus, and Pride aimed to keep it that way.

Even if it meant putting up with a mountain of a man who was in a foul mood and had a tongue as sharp as a porcupine's quill.

Pulling back Bear's long underwear, Pride dampened a cloth and washed the area over the wound gently with soap and water. Bear hissed through his teeth, but Pride had a feeling that was more for effect than actual pain.

"It's snowing outside again," Pride said, trying to make conversation. "Heavy, too. Coming in sideways. Wind's a-blowing mighty fierce. Like as not, we'll be buried by tonight." He dried Bear's chest and started to button up his long johns, but Bear slapped his hands away, doing it himself.

Bear nodded. "This time of year we get blizzards coming down off the mountains. Won't be able to set foot out of the cabin until the spring thaw, and then you need to watch out for flash floods. Snowmelt from up high on the peaks comes a-pouring down, uprooting trees and sweeping up every in its path. And Lordy, you wouldn't believe the smell! All kinds of dead varmints floating in it, stinking up everything."

"Sounds like fun, Bear. I can't hardly wait."

Bear chuckled, and the sound warmed Pride's heart.

"Well, with any luck the run-off will pass us clean by, and there won't be much picking up to do. I built the cabin on a rise because of that. Didn't want dead critters piling up outside my door."

"Good thinking. How's your arm feeling today? Can

you move it more?"

Bear slowly lifted his arm up, wincing a bit. "Yeah, it's getting on fine. Be happier when you quit babying me, though. I got us a checker set to finish whittling."

"Just give it another couple of days, Bear. That bullet was in there deep."

Bear was quiet for a few moments, staring off into the corner of the room. "You saved my life, you know," he said softly. "And after everything I said to you, too. Didn't mean none of it. Didn't really want you to go."

"I know it, Bear. I didn't want to go, either."

"Can't go now."

"Not unless I can swim through snow."

"I'm sorry that you're stuck here with me."

"I'm not," Pride said, ducking down and kissing Bear lightly. Lord, but those warm, soft lips tasted good. Felt good too, especially when they yielded against his and started kissing him back. But that made things start a-jumping in his britches, and Bear was in no condition for Pride to be thinking with his dick. He pulled away reluctantly. "Gonna fry us up some possum for supper tonight. Got roasted potatoes and corn, too, and I baked us some sourdough to go with it."

"Ain't nothing wrong with my nose, Pride. I been smelling that bread all morning," Bear groused, although his cheeks flushed and he smiled. His tongue swept over his lower lip, as if he could still taste Pride's lips on it. "You best simmer that possum a long while first, else we'll likely be chewing him all night long."

Pride smiled and stood up, gathering together the rags, bucket of water, and the soap he'd used to clean Bear's wound. "It's already done. Supper will be ready in an hour or so, I guess." He was halfway out the door when Bear spoke again.

"Pride? Thanks. For everything."

Pride nodded toward Bear. "You're welcome. Now rest yourself, you stubborn old goat, else I'm gonna have to tie you down."

"I ain't stubborn!"

"Just an old goat, huh?"

"Oh, you are in for a world of trouble when you finally let me get out of this bed, boy."

"Promise?" Pride laughed, leaving the alcove. He was still chuckling as he banged around near the stove, pulling out the freshly baked loaf of sourdough bread and checking on the possum.

As time went on it was obvious that being wounded had done nothing to diminish Bear's appetite. As a matter of fact, as he'd healed, it seemed it had gotten even heartier than it had been before he'd been shot. That night alone he'd already swallowed whole two heaping plates of venison stew, a half a loaf of sourdough bread and two cups of coffee, and he wasn't done yet. Ignoring Pride's raised brow, he'd held his plate out for a third helping.

"If you eat much more, your gut is likely to bust wide open," Pride chided, shaking his head at Bear as he watched him sop up the last drops of gravy with a thick slice of sourdough.

"Don't need to worry none about that," Bear said, sitting back. "I'm done. Couldn't eat another bite." He belched long and loud, patting his stomach. "'Scuse me," he grinned. "That stew sure stuck to my ribs good."

"With all you ate, it ain't *stuck* to your ribs -- it's *wedged* in there tight."

Laughing, Bear pushed himself away from the table, picking up both of their plates. For a while he busied himself cleaning up, scraping and washing the plates along with the stew pot.

That was the deal. If Pride cooked, then Bear cleaned, and he wouldn't give an inch about it, wounded shoulder or no. They'd had a few loud to-dos over it, especially in the beginning when his wound had been fresh, but Bear wouldn't have it any other way. The minute Pride had let him out of his bed for longer than it took him to pee, he'd stood firm on it. He smiled to himself remembering Pride going toe-to-toe with him, the top of his head barely reaching Bear's chin as he had yelled up at Bear to leave the dishes be and rest his shoulder.

Try as he might, Bear couldn't intimidate Pride by his size alone. Pride was small, but his backbone was tempered steel and Bear had to admit that he admired his gumption, pure and simple. He submitted to Pride's fussing over his shoulder, and secretly enjoyed the attention no matter how loudly he protested, but he wouldn't allow Pride to do all the work once Bear was up and around. They'd butted heads over it, and there'd been a few times when Bear was certain that Pride would have loved to have tanned his hide had he been able, but eventually he'd come to see it Bear's way.

Sitting back down at the table, he glanced at the sixty-four small squares of black and red that Pride had painstakingly painted on the top of it. Pride had already set up the twenty-four wooden checkers that Bear had whittled for them, ready for their nightly game. Half of the pieces had been carved with a strikingly realistic grizzly in their center, the other half with a mountain lion.

"Your move," Pride said, pouring them each a couple of fingers of whiskey from Bear's jug.

"I'm thinking."

"Think faster. I ain't getting any younger, Bear."

"Got someplace you need to be?" Bear chuckled, raising a brow at Pride. He was being prickly tonight, and Bear didn't know why. "Maybe you ain't looked outside lately, but we're snowed in. Ain't neither of us gonna be promenading anywhere but to bed tonight."

Pride froze, then turned away with a jerk to replace the jug of whiskey back into the cupboard.

Bear narrowed his eyes at the flush that had crept up the back of Pride's neck. "Now, what in tarnation is wrong with you, boy? We don't need to play if you ain't up to it. You're the one who set up the board."

"It's fine."

"It ain't fine. You've got a bug up your bottom about something, Pride. What did I do?"

"Nothing," Pride said curtly, sitting down opposite Bear. His fingers idly traced the mountain lion carved on his playing pieces, and he wouldn't meet Bear's eyes.

"Nothing my ass."

"Just move, Bear."

Bear frowned, but slid one of his pieces up a square. They were both silent as they played, until finally Bear had had enough. "You done made one stupid move after another, Pride. You're not even trying. You let me set up for a triple jump just now! Might as well just *give* me your pieces and be done with it."

Pride didn't say anything, just tossed back the remainder of his whiskey in one long swallow.

"What's gotten into you? C'mon Pride, talk to me. You got me worried now. Ain't like you to throw a game like this."

"Guess I'm just tired, is all. Gonna get to bed, Bear," Pride said softly. He stacked his checkers into a neat pile, then picked up a lantern and walked into the alcove, sitting down on the far side of the bed, his back to Bear.

Bear watched him for a few minutes as Pride pulled off his boots, pants and shirt and lay down on the bed in his long johns, pulling the quilt up to his chin. Something was wrong. Powerful wrong. Pride *never* passed on the chance to whoop Bear's butt in checkers. He *never* went to bed early, and he sure as shit was *never* as quiet as he'd been all night.

Walking into the alcove, Bear stripped to his underwear and sat down. "Pride?"

"What?"

"You feeling okay?"

"I'm fine."

"Stop saying that. You're not fine," Bear grumbled, crossing his arms over his broad chest and frowning.

"Okay... I'm *not* fine. Happy?" Pride shot back, as he rolled over, turning his back to Bear.

"What's wrong?"

"Nothing."

"Damn it, Pride! Just tell me what I did wrong!"

"You didn't do anything wrong, Bear. Told you that afore."

Bear laid his hand on Pride's shoulder, ignoring his attempt to shrug it off, and forced him to roll onto his back so he could see Pride's face. "You're lying to me, Pride. Be better if you hauled off and whomped me a good one upside the head than lie to me," he said, cupping Pride's prickly chin with his fingers.

Pride sprang up like someone had lit a fire in his britches, throwing back the quilt and sitting on the edge of the bed, his back once again to Bear. His head hung down low, and he ran his fingers through his hair. He hadn't cut it since he'd come to the cabin, and it fell to brush his shoulders in a wild tangle of corn silk. "Please don't touch me, Bear."

"What? Why? You got a toothache?" Bear asked, wondering if his fingers on Pride's jaw had been what had made him bounce out of bed like he'd done.

"No, that ain't what aches."

"Pride, if you don't just up and tell me what's wrong

with you, I swear I'm gonna pitch you out headfirst through the window into the snow."

"I've been thinking about you, Bear, all right? That's all. Now leave me be."

"Thinking about what?"

"*You*."

"I ain't deaf, Pride. You done said that already. What about me?"

Pride twisted around and looked over his shoulder at Bear. His dark eyes flashed with a look that Bear hadn't seen since before he'd been shot.

He didn't say a word, but that look told Bear exactly what was troubling Pride, and it was something a lot further south than his teeth.

Bear bit back a grin. He was so relieved that he wasn't sure if he wanted to laugh, or punch Pride square in the face for making him worry. "Damnation, Pride, why didn't you just say so?" he asked softly. He stroked the side of Pride's face with one finger, lazily trailing it down over Pride's stubbly cheek.

"Didn't think you wanted that, Bear," Pride said softly, closing his eyes. "After the argument we had before you was shot, I thought we was done with it. Since your shoulder healed, you ain't made a move to... "

"Done told you already that I didn't mean nothing I said back then. And how was I supposed to know that *you* wanted it? Shit, we sleep together in the same bed every damned night. We say goodnight and you roll over and that's that. You ain't kissed me since just after I was shot."

"That's 'cause you ain't *never* kissed me."

"I've wanted to, but I didn't think you was interested," Bear said softly. "Thought maybe that first time was only because you were grateful that I saved you from that mountain lion." He sighed, brushing a wayward hank of hair from Pride's eyes. "If you want to know the truth, I think about you all the time. About that one night we had...about how good it felt. I want that again. Want it real bad, Pride."

Pride blinked and looked down at his hands, then turned lust-filled, hopeful eyes up at Bear. "Me, too," he whispered.

Bear swallowed hard, feeling his throat choke up. Trouble was, while he wanted Pride in the worst way, he just wasn't sure how to go about satisfying the itch that was clawing at his belly. Had to be more to it than just the rubbing they done the last time. He decided it would be best to trust his gut. It had never let him down before.

Grabbing Pride's chin with his fingers, he leaned in and kissed him hard, hungrily. The need that had been boiling in his belly, and that Bear had kept squashing, exploded to the surface as he plundered Pride's soft lips. But when Pride reached for him, Bear pushed him away.

"Stand up, Pride."

"What?" Pride blinked, cocking his head at Bear as if he hadn't quite understood him.

"I said, *stand up*," Bear growled. His gut was telling him to take charge, and that was exactly what he was going to do.

Chapter Ten

Hesitantly, Pride did as Bear had ordered him. He stood up and looked down at Bear, feeling his cheeks heat up, his lips burning from Bear's kiss. Confused, he blinked at Bear, not understanding what was going through the man's mind. He'd never seen Bear act like this before -- commanding and forceful, the tone of his voice warning Pride not to disobey. Pride's head wasn't sure that he liked Bear's tone at all, but his dick was of a different opinion. It jumped against the wool of his long johns, hard and ready.

"Strip down, boy."

"Bear... "

"*Strip down.* I want to see you, Pride -- *all* of you." Bear scooted to rest his back against the headboard of the bed, folding his arms behind his head. His eyes were hooded and dark with lust as he watched Pride from under his thick lashes. "Slow, now. *Real* slow."

Pride's voice failed him and he was hesitant to respond to Bear's command. He'd had his fill of a lifetime of following orders. But he realized that this was different, and the difference was that he trusted Bear and wanted to please him. After only a few heartbeats his fingers slid to the top button of his long johns, slowly working it free. He felt odd – nervous, a little embarrassed, and excited, all at the same time.

Bear's eyes were heated, riveted to the skin Pride was exposing bit-by-bit. They were searing Pride no less than if Bear's fingers had been stroking his skin, and soon had Pride so hard that he worried for a minute that he might come in his underwear before he even got the opportunity to touch Bear.

The second button slipped free.

Pride had to fight the urge to crawl up on the bed and kiss Bear blind, to rip his long johns off and taste every inch of him. Parting his lips, his tongue peeked out from between them as if he could taste Bear from across the room. Bear's moan and his softly uttered oath, as well as the lump that was lengthening between his thighs encouraged Pride. Fine. If Bear wanted a show, then Pride would give him one. He let his lips curve into a knowing, teasing smile as he popped the third and fourth buttons free.

His long johns gaped open down to his bellybutton, exposing his chest. He looked down at himself, then flicked his eyes up at Bear. His tongue swept over his bottom lip as Pride ran his hands over his smooth skin, teasing his nipples into hard peaks under his callused fingertips.

"Goddamn, Pride..." Bear breathed. His hands were fisted at his sides, his muscles tense, and there was no mistaking the thick, hard bulge that had risen under his woolens.

"Like that, huh?" Pride grinned, loving what he was doing to Bear's body. He looked every bit as hard and ready as Pride, and Pride hadn't even touched him yet. Just *looking* at Pride was making Bear's cock rise. The thought pleased Pride and made his erection twitch eagerly as he slid his arms free from the sleeves of his long johns, letting the gray fabric hang loose around his lean hips.

Turning his back to Bear, Pride looked at him once over his shoulder, then slowly inched his 'johns down over his hips, baring his ass. Pulling them free of his feet, he tossed them over his shoulder and across the bed, hitting Bear in the face.

Bear clawed them off, his eyes wide and his breath quickening. Peeking over his shoulder again, Pride saw that Bear's eyes were glued to his rear end. Teasingly, Pride ran his hands around his hips and over his ass, wiggling a bit and thrusting his butt out in Bear's direction.

His cock was fully erect and glistening with moisture at its tip when Pride finally turned around. He kept his eyes on Bear as he brushed his fingers through the crisp dark brown hair that nested it. Rubbing his thumb over the head, he slicked himself before wrapping his fingers around the thick shaft.

Pride had no idea that Bear could move as fast as he did. He dang near shot off the bed, stripping out of his own underwear at lightning speed. Bear's cock was every bit as thick and long as Pride remembered, a dick worthy of a mountain of a man. Before Bear could lift a finger to touch him, Pride dropped to his knees, and took hold of it with both hands.

"Lord, Bear…" Pride whispered hoarsely, his breath ghosting over the head of Bear's erection. His tongue flicked out, swirling over the rounded head. Pulling back the foreskin, he sucked the tip into his mouth. Bear's musky flavor and scent filled his senses, making his heart race, his head whirl, and his cock bob with jealousy.

"Pride!" Bear groaned, his fingers twisting in Pride's hair. "What are you doing? Oh, God, Pride… Don't stop…please, Pride, don't you dare stop."

Pride raised his eyes to meet Bear's as he drew Bear's

length deeply into his throat. He tasted Bear's essence on his tongue, thick, salty drops that told Pride Bear wasn't going to last much longer. Releasing his cock from his mouth, Pride looked up at Bear. "I'm gonna make you come, Bear. Make you come so hard that you're gonna see every star in the Colorado skies. Gonna drain you dry," he said, grinning. "And then I'm going to fuck you."

"You're gonna *w-what*? H-how...ohh..." Bear stammered, but his question lowered into a long, low moan as Pride sucked him in deep again. One hand slipped low to cup Bear's balls, rock-hard and furry, while the other held his cock firm, squeezing gently as Pride's lips slid over his length. He grazed the delicate skin with his teeth, drawing a hiss from Bear, and smiled around Bear's girth.

He released Bear only long enough to quickly stick a finger in his mouth, wetting it, before capturing Bear's cock with his lips again. His slicked finger slid between Bear's legs to his ass, tracing the crack before slipping in between. In Pride's opinion, there wasn't anything more intimate than touching a man's asshole, rubbing against the hidden, ridged flesh that nobody else, not even the man himself, got to see.

Bear seemed to be beyond noticing, though. He was groaning louder now, rocking his hips and fucking Pride's mouth. Pride didn't really need to do anything but sit still as Bear took over doing all the work. Instead, Pride concentrated on wiggling his fingertip inside of Bear's body bit-by-bit, pushing it past the tight ring of muscle and deeply into Bear's silken channel. Lord! It was as hot as an inferno in there, and thinking of sliding his cock in deep rather than his finger nearly had Pride coming undone. He realized that he needed Bear to finish up right quick, or else Pride was never going to last long enough to get the opportunity.

Curling his finger, he hit Bear's gland, and sucked harder on his cock.

Bear roared as he came, his hands cupping either side of Pride's head tightly, his washboard stomach tightening further, rippling with the force of his orgasm.

Pride drank every drop, then licked Bear clean as he finally finished shuddering, the muscles in his thighs trembling. He crawled up Bear's body, sliding his hands over the hard muscles of his legs, stomach, and chest, then cupped Bear's cheeks and kissed him hungrily. Pride's cock dug into Bear's hip, hard and dripping with his need. "I got a powerful need to be inside you, Bear," he whispered, nibbling at Bear's lower lip.

"How?" Bear asked, although his eyes remained closed and a slight, sated smile played at the corners of his mouth.

"You don't need to do nothing but lay back," Pride said, guiding Bear to the bed. "Lay down, Bear. I'll be right back." He raced into the kitchen, hoping that he wouldn't find Bear fast asleep by the time he got back.

Reaching the cupboard, he pulled the tin container of lard down off the shelf and carried it with him back into the alcove. He was prying open the lid before he even reached Bear's side.

Bear wasn't asleep, but he wasn't far from it. His eyes were heavy, straining to remain open, his cheeks still flushed from his pleasure and his forehead dotted with sweat. "Bear?" Pride said, crawling onto the bed, setting the tin of lard down to the side and nudging Bear's legs apart. He knelt between them, running his hands over the tight muscles of Bear's thighs. "Lordy, you are a beautiful man."

Bear chuckled, reaching up to stroke Pride's cheek. "Liar. I'm a big ol' lump of hair that learned how to walk and talk."

Pride leaned down over Bear's face, his eyes hard and flashing. "Not to me. Look what you done to me, boy, and you ain't even touched me." He thrust his cock against the skin of Bear's stomach, shivering as the hair that covered it tickled at his foreskin. "You got me so hard my dick's likely bust open at the seams if I don't do something about it soon." His expression softened, and he leaned down for a gentle kiss. "Do you trust me, Bear?"

"'Course I trust you. You saved my life, Pride."

"Yeah, but do you *really* trust me?"

"You go on and do whatever it is you got a mind to do, Pride. I trust you."

Pride felt tears sting his eyes, but blinked them back. He kissed Bear again, lying flush against his body. Bear's arms wrapped around him, and his hands roamed over the skin of Pride's back, down to his ass. He groaned as Bear's fingers kneaded the flesh of his behind, and felt his body harden until it was strung as tight as catgut on a fiddle.

Pushing himself away, Pride licked and nipped his way down Bear's body, taking a few minutes to worship Bear's cock again. Softened, it tasted of Bear's spent seed as he rolled his tongue over it. Letting it be, Pride nibbled at the sensitive skin over Bear's hipbones, then traced the deep cleft between Bear's thigh and his balls with his tongue. Bear's cock was twitching, waking up again, and it brought another rush of heat to Pride's groin.

He couldn't have waited another moment if both of their lives had depended on it. Rearing between Bear's legs, he spread Bear's legs and bent his knees.

Puckered sienna flesh ringed with black hair beckoned to him from between Bear's cheeks. Dipping down, he flicked his tongue over the pebbled hole, curling his tongue and pushing in a bit. Bear began moaning, his hands fisting in the quilt that covered the bed, but he sounded far away to Pride. He was too overcome with his own lust and need to be aware of anything other than the musky taste that filled his mouth and the thudding of his own blood in his veins.

Grabbing the jar of lard, he scooped out a healthy helping and coated his rock-hard dick with it. The cool grease did nothing to lessen the pulsing ache that had him baring his teeth and growling like a wolf in rut. He coated Bear's asshole for good measure, slipping a finger in up to the knuckle. The silky walls of Bear's channel tightened around his finger, and his cock jumped in response.

Pride hissed through his teeth. "Lordy, Bear, you're as tight as a miser's fist," he whispered, slipping another finger in next to the first. Flicking his eyes up, he saw that Bear had taken his cock in his hand, slowly stroking the hardening flesh of a reawakening erection. Bear's eyes were screwed shut, and he was biting his lower lip. "Am I hurting you, Bear?" Pride asked. The last thing he wanted was to cause this man pain.

"If you stop, I may have to kill you," Bear growled, not opening his eyes. Pride grinned, leaning down and trailing his tongue over Bear's balls. He sucked one into his mouth, rolling it over with his tongue until Bear was practically purring and riding his two fingers. When he released Bear's sac from his mouth, it was to a deeply disappointed growl from Bear.

Rising between Bear's thighs, Pride took himself in hand and pressed the head of his erection against Bear's asshole. Slick with lard and his own juices, he slowly, carefully, pushed himself inside Bear's body.

Pride wasn't as large as Bear, but he wasn't a small man in that respect either, and Bear's eyes popped open as his cock slid deeply into his ass, stretching him, filling him up. Pride pushed in to the root, until he was fully encased in the fiery, satiny channel within Bear's body.

Two bodies united. Two men made one. The thought was humbling, and made Pride's chest tighten with emotions that were foreign to him. Feelings that made his eyes burn with the strength of them, feelings like belonging, compassion, and love.

"Pride? You're in me, ain't you...inside of me?" Bear whispered, groaning as he stroked himself.

"Yeah, I am. Filled you up, Bear. You feel so good, so damn fucking good," Pride moaned. He pulled himself nearly completely out of Bear's body, then slid himself back in to the hilt, moving faster as the pressure built up in his balls. The pleasure of pushing himself deeply into Bear's body, knowing no one had ever gone there before was nearly unbearable. He teetered on the edge of release, and as he watched Bear come again, this time over his own fist, he toppled over the edge.

He came so hard that he saw stars, his vision dimming for a moment as he spurted deeply into Bear's body. Riding the crest of a wave of ecstasy unlike any he'd experienced before, Pride's back arched and every muscle in his body tightened and strained from its intensity. Finally emptied, he slumped down on top of Bear, his cock slowly softening and sliding out.

"Good God, Pride," Bear said, wrapping his arms around Pride's back, crushing him to his chest. "I never knew a body could make a man feel like that. I felt...like I was a part of you. Or you was a part of me. Or, hell, I don't know...*something*."

"I know, Bear. Me, too. Never felt that way with nobody afore. Just with you," Pride said truthfully. He kissed Bear's chest, then laid his cheek against it. "Never thought I'd find anybody who made me feel this way."

"Me neither. Pride?"

"Yeah?"

"I don't want you to leave come spring. I want you to stay."

Pride lifted his head, looking into Bear's eyes. Bear's face looked hopeful and at the same time a little scared, as if he were a-feared that Pride would say no. Pride swallowed hard, feeling his eyes burn again. "I don't want to leave, Bear. There ain't nothing I want more in this world than to stay put right here in this cabin, with you."

"Good. It's settled then," Bear said, laying his head back and closing his eyes. He sighed happily.

Pride smiled, closing his eyes. They were both covered in semen, sticky and sweaty, lying half-on, half-off the bed, and the quilt was a bunched-up mess, but it would've taken an army to pull them apart. Pride was staying put -- for the night and, if he and Bear had their way, forever.

Chapter Eleven

Pride and Bear leaned over the kitchen table, Bear's map spread out before them. Their heads were so close together that they bumped noggins every time one or the other of them moved.

Outside the cabin, rain sluiced against the dovetailed logs in a never-ending patter. Spring had come, but it had arrived wet, bringing with it torrential downpours that had turned the hills around the cabin into a soggy, muddy mess. Between the rain and the snowmelt, they might as well have been living in the middle of a lake.

"I don't know these hills, Bear. Ain't there anything out there that looks like a skull to you? Or could be that it's some old Indian burial mound," Pride asked, tracing his finger around the black mark near the center of the map. "Seen a few of those on my way here from Texas."

"Not that I can remember," Bear answered, shaking his head. "I done told you I been all over these foothills, but ain't never found nothing."

"Well, you got a fresh pair of eyes to go scouting with you this time," Pride smiled.

Bear grinned, leaning over the map and pressing his lips to Pride's gently. He loved the taste of Pride, never tired of it, and wanted it more and more as the winter had worn on. He never passed up the opportunity to kiss him, to touch him, and likely as not one kiss would lead to another, and then another, until they both ended up sweating and spent.

It was a fine life as far as Bear was concerned, and he was happier than he could ever before recall being.

Not that they didn't butt heads. They did. All the time, it seemed, and over everything from their nightly checker games to whose turn it was to cook supper.

"I cooked yesterday, Bear."

"No, you didn't neither. I made that rabbit stew."

"Yeah, well...I had to eat it."

Lordy, but the man could be irritating. And sweet. And gentle. And sexy enough to put a tent in Bear's underwear every damned time he looked at him.

The good thing about their frequent arguments was that every time they locked horns, they kissed and made up right after. Bear smiled to himself, silently admitting that sometimes he picked a fight for just that reason. Although he'd never said so and Bear had never asked, he was fairly sure that Pride did the same.

"Wish this rain would let up," Pride said, as he stood up and arched his back, stretching. "I'm getting cabin fever."

"Yeah, it's a wet one, ain't it? But it's still real early in the season, Pride. It's bitter-cold up on the mountains. The snow ain't melted up there yet, and when it does we could be in for flash floods. Could be dangerous to go out too far now, anyhow."

"Sure would be nice to get some fresh meat, though. 'Course, with the way it's been raining and all, we could just chuck a line out of the window and catch us some fish."

Bear laughed, nodding. "Ain't that the truth? Well, I

suppose next time the rain stops we could go a-hunting, if we don't wander too far and stick to the high ground."

Pride beamed a smile at him that warmed Bear's heart and groin at the same time. He had a grin on him that tickled Bear deep inside, and always made Bear want to smile back. And then do other things -- things that involved the two of them getting naked and sweaty.

Bear's first taste of Pride had come soon after that first night they'd made love for good and real. His cock had been hard, a red-hot poker that had scalded Bear's entire body when it had touched his tongue. He liked the taste of Pride, hungered for it like a drunkard yearned for whiskey. Couldn't go long without it, before he was feeling knotted up and needy inside. Luckily for Bear, Pride didn't seem to mind him groping at him at all hours of the day and night.

He leaned in and cupped Pride's scruffy cheek in his palm, kissing him again…and again.

For the next long while, neither one of them gave a single thought to the rain, to hunting, or to the map that lay abandoned on the kitchen table. In short order, they were well on their way to getting sweaty and spent.

A shot rang out in the stillness of the forest, rolling across the hills, echoing on and on. The elk dropped to its knees and, with a mournful bellow, fell to its side and lay still.

"Whoo-hoo! A twelve-pointer, Bear! Look at that rack!" Pride shouted as the two men ran across the mucky clearing, mud sucking at the soles of their boots, to where the elk lay. They hunkered down next to the carcass, examining the beast. "Good clean kill, Bear. Nice thick pelt, too."

"Yeah. Still got its winter coat. Later on in the season

they get too scruffy-looking to bother with, unless you want to make buckskin," Bear said, pulling his fingers through the soft fur of the elk. "Well, we'd best get busy, unless you want to drag this sumbitch all the way back to the cabin. Bastard must weigh in at eight hundred pounds or so. Figure we should butcher it here. Take the best cuts, and the hide, maybe the rack. Bring them home, leave the rest."

Pride nodded, pulled out his knife and straddled the elk, slitting its throat. He cut through the elk's tender underside, from its throat to its anus, and Bear set about cleaning it out. Pride made the necessary cuts to remove the hide once Bear had the elk cleaned and the sweetmeats set aside.

They'd just removed the hide and had begun hacking out the cuts of meat that they preferred, when a strange rumbling sound reached them and tremors vibrated through the ground beneath their feet. Pride looked to Bear in confusion, but one glimpse at the fear frozen on Bear's face made his gut wrench.

Bear's eyes were scanning the higher hills that sat flush against the towering, jagged mountains, and he'd turned pale. "Pride!" he cried, bolting to his feet.

The rumbling was swiftly growing louder. Pride looked in the direction Bear had been staring, and saw that something was crashing down the mountainside and heading straight for them. It cut through the trees of the dense forest that carpeted the hills, moving faster than anything Pride had ever seen before. It was as if some invisible giant were racing toward them, snapping trees under its feet as if they were no more than twigs.

"What in the hell is it, Bear?" Pride demanded, feeling his heart begin to hammer in his chest.

"Flash flood! Run!" Bear cried. He dropped his knife, reaching over and roughly pulling Pride up by the arm.

"Got to get to higher ground!"

Tearing through the brush, Bear and Pride raced through the wood as the rumble behind them grew into a roar that shook the very earth.

Ahead of them was an outcrop of rock that rose at least fifteen feet high, and Bear headed straight for it. Scaling the gray stones, they reached the top just as the leading edge of a frothy wave of water crashed through the brush behind them, the spray exploding over the rock, drenching them both.

The stone shuddered as the wave of muddied water battered it, parting around the outcrop, only momentarily inconvenienced by the solid rock. The floodwaters flowed together on the other side, never losing an ounce of their devastating power. Ripping up brush and uprooting trees, the mighty whitewaters swept along nearly everything that stood in their path with a deafening roar.

The sound was loud enough to make them both cover their ears as they knelt on the flat, cold stone of the top of the outcrop, watching the waters crash by. In a swirling, foaming river of mud, logs, and animal carcasses -- including their elk – the flood tumbled over itself as it raced downhill to the Snake River that lay far below. Eventually it would bloat the river to overflowing its banks, flooding the lowlands.

Pride had never seen anything like it before. The rivers he'd crossed during his travels may have been wide and deep, like the Mississippi, but they'd been lazy, keeping to their banks peacefully. What flowed beneath his feet was a monster, a force that a man couldn't fight, couldn't stand against. He shuddered to think of what would have happened to them if the stone outcrop hadn't been as close as it was. His and Bear's bodies would have been among the carcasses being swept away.

It seemed to take forever for the onslaught to end, until

the waters ebbed and finally passed them by. The flood left the area around the outcrop a sodden mess, with deep pockets of standing water that reeked of earth, dampness, and death. Carcasses and brush had piled against the side of the outcrop, grisly gifts left behind by the surging waters.

"Lost my Bowie," Bear grumbled, peering over the edge of the outcrop, surveying the damage.

"Your knife? Shit, we damn near lost our hides, Bear," Pride chuckled, although his heart still pounded. "Guess we can get you another Bowie next time we go down to St. Elmo's. Providing there's a St. Elmo's to get to, of course."

"She'll be there. Ain't the first flood the mountains spat out."

"So, what do we do now?"

"Head back to the cabin, I guess."

Pride nodded and stood up. "Sure is a shame to lose that elk, though. He was a beauty," he said, looking down at the broad face of the outcrop. His head tilted to the side and he took a step backwards, then turned slowly in a circle. "Bear? Looky here... "

"What?"

"Look at the shape this rock takes."

Bear stepped to stand next to Pride, both men staring down at the top of the gray stone outcrop. The front part was wide and rounded, the rear narrowing and squaring. Two deep, roughly circular indents lay side-by-side in the center, creasing the otherwise smooth rock face.

"A body could almost think that this looked like a skull, Bear," Pride said. "And it would be about where that mark is on your map, ain't it?"

"Yeah, that it would. Could be you're right," Bear replied. "But this ain't the time to be worrying about no treasure, Pride. We got to get back to the cabin, and it ain't gonna be easy slugging through that mess down there. I ain't looking forward to it."

"Guess you're right, Bear. Still and all, it makes a body wonder. You think you'll be able to find this place again?"

"This ain't the first time I've seen it, Pride. That's how I knew to run here when the floodwaters broke. I just ain't never climbed it afore."

Pride grinned, his eyes lighting up with excitement. "We're gonna find your Pa's treasure, Bear. I just know it."

Bear laughed, shaking his head at Pride's enthusiasm. "Could be. But I ain't a-hunting for treasure now. All I'm gonna be looking for tonight is a nice hot meal and a warm bath."

"I hear that," Pride laughed. His grin widened and he looked at Bear slyly. "Maybe do some treasure-hunting under the quilt after?"

"Now *that* kind of hunting you can do all you want, Pride," Bear grinned. "And you don't need no map to find it, neither. Now, come on. It's gonna take us a long while to get back, and I'd like to get home afore dark."

Carefully picking their way down the side of the outcrop, they reached the bottom, their boots sinking deeply into the mud left behind by the flood.

Pride pulled one of his feet free with an effort, the cold mud sucking hard at his boot. It popped free with a *pukkah* sound, and sunk in just as deeply with the next step he took. Bear was right. It was going to take them a heap of time to waddle through the mess. The mud sucked his boot right off his foot with his next step, and he had to fish it out of the mud.

Taking off his other boot, he opted to stay barefoot, although his feet froze in the ice-cold mud. Still, it made his progress easier, and Bear followed suit. The two men slowly slogged through the mud, skirting the debris left behind by the floodwaters, until they finally made their way past the wide swath of destruction and reached dry ground.

By the time they reached the cabin they were chilled to the bone, their teeth chattering, their feet blue with the cold, their bodies shaking, and it was all Pride could do to hold his hands steady long enough to light a fire. Bear filled the coffee pot with water and grounds, and set it over the flames before running into the alcove and snatching the quilt from the bed and the jug from the cupboard.

Stripped naked, the quilt wrapped tightly around the two of them, they sat on the floor close to the fire, letting the flames slowly warm them. Passing the jug back and forth between them, they each drank deeply, the whiskey warming their stomachs. By the time the coffee was boiling, they'd both thawed out enough to feel the heat of each other's skin against their own.

Pride slid his hand over Bear's chest, brushing his fingertips through the hair that covered it. Lifting the edge of the quilt, he leaned over and licked at one of Bear's umber-colored nipples, swirling his tongue over the stiffening peak.

"For crying out loud, Pride -- I'm covered in mud and so are you, and we both stink like a cornered skunk," Bear growled, although his lips curled in a lazy smile and he closed his eyes, tipping his head back.

"Mmm, don't taste like skunk," Pride murmured against his chest, kissing his way up across the warmed flesh to Bear's exposed throat. He pulled the tender skin between his teeth, nipping lightly.

"And how would you know what skunk tasted like?"

Bear chuckled, pushing Pride away. "We both need to wash up. Go on and fetch us a bucket of water, and I'll stoke the fire."

Grumbling at being thwarted, Pride stood up, letting the quilt fall to his feet. His cock was erect, and he palmed it slowly. "Looky at what you done, Bear. Ain't right to get a man all worked up like this and then turn your nose up at him."

"You're the one that's got yourself all worked up, and if you keep on like that there ain't gonna be nothing left for me to do. Now turn yourself loose and go fetch that water," Bear laughed, swatting Pride's leg. He stood up, his own erection thickening against his thigh.

Pride eyed it meaningfully. "Not the only one who's got himself riled up," he grinned. "Tell you what, Bear. I'll fetch the water and when it's done heating, I'll wash your back for you."

"I ain't about to turn my back to you with you being as randy as a hound dog in heat," Bear laughed.

"You never complained before."

"You was never this dirty before."

Pride growled, but padded away to collect the bucket as Bear had ordered. Throwing his elk skin coat over his naked body, he slipped outside and ran lightly around the corner of the cabin to the rain barrel. Dipping the bucket inside, he lifted it back out brimming with clear, cold rainwater and carried it carefully back inside the cabin.

Chapter Twelve

Bear was on his hands and knees, poking at the fire. The sight of his rounded buttocks bared to the cool air of the cabin, dark hair dusting the crack and the heavy sac that hung between his muscular thighs, heated Pride's groin no less quickly than if he'd jumped straight into the flames prick-first.

He looked at Pride over his shoulder, his thick black hair gleaming in the firelight. "You gonna close that door or just lay out the welcome mat for every critter in the forest to come on in?" he grumbled, turning back to the fire. Pride swore that Bear lifted his butt just a little bit higher into the air as he stirred the logs with an iron poker.

Frowning, Pride banged the door shut with his foot. Carrying the bucket over to the hearth, he tried not to slosh too much water over the sides on to the plank floor. "You keep shoving that ass of yours into the air and, stink or no stink, I'm gonna be on you like white on rice, Bear," he growled, pouring water from the bucket into the pot Bear had set out. Lifting the pot, he hung it from the hook over the fire. "Only so much a man can take before he breaks."

Bear chuckled, sitting back on his heels. "A man would think you hadn't gotten laid in a dog's age, 'stead of just yesterday, Pride."

"Yeah, well...almost getting drowned will do that to me every damned time." Pride sat down on the floor next to Bear, watching the water in the pot slowly start to steam. "That flood sure was something, though, wasn't it? Thought for sure that we was going to be doing the backstroke clear to Heaven. Thank God you knew where that outcrop was, Bear."

"Told you I know these hills like the back of my hand. Sure were a scary couple of minutes though. That water moves faster than lightning, and there ain't nothing stopping it."

"Yeah. But it was funny how the water took some trees and left others standing, ain't it?"

"It's only the trees that bend that don't get ripped up," Bear said quietly. "Kind of like people. A body can't survive who can't bend and roll with what life throws at 'em."

"Ain't that the truth," Pride said, nodding. He shouldered Bear, a sly grin creasing his cheeks. "Know what I'd like to see bending right now?"

"What?"

"You, over the bed."

"Lordy, I never met a man with such a one-track mind as you, Pride," Bear snorted, shaking his head. "You ever think with anything 'sides your dick?"

"Yeah, but the thoughts in my head ain't near as much fun."

Bear laughed, his rich baritone voice tickling Pride deep in his belly, making him want him even more. "Be a few days until the ground soaks up that water. But I'm itching to get back up there. Can't believe that in all these years I ain't never realized that those rocks were shaped like a skull," Bear said, when his laughter had died down.

"Like you said, you never climbed up there afore. No way for you to know." Pride sighed and stood up, walking over to the table and spreading out Bear's map. He had to move, do something, *anything* to get his mind off Bear's muscular, naked, and all-too-tempting body. Damn, he could barely think straight, what with his balls swelled up like they were. If Pride had his way, this was going to be the fastest bath in history.

"If this here mark is that outcrop, then that would put the "X" about a half mile northwest, just past whatever this squiggly line is supposed to be," he said, pointing to another black smudge on the map. "Now, this mark next to the "X" looks like a tombstone, Bear. Maybe whoever buried the treasure marked it like a grave. Next time we go out we ought to carry a pickaxe and a shovel with us. Just in case," he said.

"That's a good idea. Best put that map away now, Pride. The water's hot," Bear said, removing the pot from the fire. He spread several thick hides on the floor, then picked up a wedge of strong-smelling soap and a rag. "You wanna go first or should I?"

"How about I wash you down?" Pride grinned, kneeling down next to Bear. He took the rag and the soap from Bear's hand, dipping the rag into the hot water. Rubbing the soap in the rag, he worked up a thick lather. "You just stand up and be still, Bear. Let me do all the work."

"Pride... "

"Don't *Pride* me. You'll get just as clean if I do it as you would if you washed yourself. Just more fun for me this way, is all. More fun for you, too, I reckon."

Bear stood up, rising to his full six-foot three inches. Pride let his eyes wander slowly up and down his body, a long, pleasurable trip. Naked and backlit by the flames,

Bear was solid wall of muscle and sinew; powerful, almost godlike.

His face was shadowed as he looked down at Pride, but Pride knew every nook and cranny of it as well as he knew his own. Rising to his feet, as Pride began to gently wash him he realized how well he'd come to know Bear.

Pride knew that small, thin scar that creased high on Bear's right cheekbone; knew the small pockmark that marred the skin along the left side of his jaw. Knew that his right ear was just a tiny bit lower than his left, nothing that a body would notice right off, but enough so that Bear was self conscious about it and wore his hair long to cover it. Pride knew that deep cleft in his chin; knew how it felt to tickle at it with his tongue.

His broad, heavily muscled shoulders spoke of Bear's hard life living alone in the hills, of his years of chopping wood and toting heavy burdens without the help of anyone else, Pride thought as he slid the soapy washcloth slowly over Bear's skin. Poor man had been alone even longer than Pride had, and Pride's heart ached for him.

His biceps were defined and rock hard, his forearms were sinewy and brawny. Even his fingers were thick and strong, but Pride knew the gentleness in them; had felt their tender touch on his skin.

There was gentleness in Bear's heart, too, Pride thought, as the wet rag brushed across his wide chest, slicking the black hair that covered it. Big enough to crack a man in half with his bare hands without breaking a sweat, Pride knew that Bear would never lift a finger against anyone who hadn't done him harm first.

Slowly he brought the rag down over Bear's washboard stomach, and Pride smiled as he wondered again how Bear could have such a ravenous appetite and not have a single ounce of fat on his body. Just pure muscle, ridged and hard, that made Pride want to touch him all day everyday.

He skirted Bear's groin, saving the best for last. Instead, he washed Bear's legs, gliding the soapy washcloth over his massive thighs and sculpted calves, his graceful -- if overly large -- feet. One at a time, he lifted them, cleaning the tops and soles, and between each toe.

With a hand on Bear's lean hip, Pride urged him to turn around so that he could wash his backside. And what a glorious backside it was, too.

The same fine black hair that covered most of the rest of Bear dusted his rear end, a bit thicker between the rounded globes. Spreading his asscheeks, Pride's tongue followed behind the washcloth, tasting Bear's unique flavor along with the soap. When Bear leaned forward and gripped the mantle, moaning, Pride just smiled and continued on.

He followed the graceful curve of Bear's spine up to his neck, washing each inch of the golden skin that hugged his finely muscled back. Squatting, he kissed his way back down, retracing that same path along Bear's spine. Lord, but he could kiss Bear's skin all day and all night and not tire of it. Hell, he could kiss him all *year*, and not weary of the way Bear felt, the way he tasted.

He lowered himself to his knees so that when Bear turned again Pride was face-to-face with his erection, grown hard and straight from Pride's soapy attentions.

Thick and heavy, his foreskin as smooth and soft as lambskin, in Pride's opinion Bear's cock was in keeping with the rest of him -- as strong as his body and just as beautiful. Leaning in, Pride took a deep breath, filling his lungs with Bear's musky scent. The washcloth slid between Bear's legs, gently soaping his sac and slowly sliding up the turgid flesh of his cock. Pride worked the rag from root to tip and back again, until Bear's breath became rough and ragged.

Suddenly, the rag was yanked out of Pride's hand and Bear pulled him up by his arm. Bear gathered him in his arms, his lips crushing against Pride's in a heated, open-mouthed kiss that left Pride breathless.

"My turn," Bear said gruffly as he relieved Pride of the washcloth and soap and forced himself to end their kiss. Pride could set Bear's flesh afire with a single look, but what he done to him with his hands and lips and a soapy rag was nothing short of torture. Bear was eager and willing to return the favor.

Pride was smaller than Bear, enough so as to look fragile standing next to him, but Bear knew that looks were deceiving. Pride's body was hard and wiry. He was all lean muscle and much stronger than he appeared. Bear loved his pale blond hair, soft and wavy, and so different from Bear's own thick black mane. He loved to feel it slip through his fingers, and pool around his cock when Pride took him into his mouth.

His jaw was sharp and square, and prickled with a new growth of beard that he hadn't bothered to shave in a few days. Bear slid the cloth over Pride's cheek, remembering how good his whiskers had felt rubbing against Bear's thighs.

Pride's shoulders and chest were smooth, with only a few golden brown hairs curling around his nipples. Nipples that Bear loved to tease with his teeth until Pride would wiggle beneath him. He washed each one carefully, rubbing the cloth over them until they peaked, then sucking each into his mouth and rolling his tongue over them for good measure.

Sliding the washcloth down the centerline of Pride's firmly muscled stomach, Bear followed the same path Pride had taken, avoiding Pride's cock, although it nearly killed Bear to do it. He wanted nothing more than to devour it, to suck it in deeply between his lips until he tasted Pride's seed. *Later. First things first*, Bear thought.

He washed Pride's legs, his lean thighs and firm calves, and his feet just as thoroughly as Pride had done his own. Turning Pride around, Bear took a moment to appreciate the fineness of Pride's rump. Lord, but how Bear loved that ass. Two handfuls of Heaven was how he thought of it, firm and solid, and beautiful. As he washed Pride's asshole, he couldn't resist any more than Pride had, and flicked his tongue over the rosy, ridged flesh.

His mind wandered to how Pride rode him when they made love. Bear had never taken Pride, although he'd thought on it from time to time. Now he wondered what it would be like to sink his cock into that tiny hole; wondered whether it would even fit in there. Bear was not a small man by any stretch of the imagination. His erection grew even harder as he thought about it and it took an effort of will to pull away and continue washing Pride.

Bear swept the soap and cloth up over Pride's spine, to the broadest part of his back where the myriad of crisscrossing scars spider-webbed across his skin. As it did each time, Bear looked at the history of Pride's early life that had been carved into his flesh, his stomach knotted with anger. No boy should have to feel such pain, especially not at his father's hand, no matter what he'd done. And that Pride -- sweet, kind, gentle Pride -- had suffered so for simply finding pleasure in another human being made it all the worse, as far as Bear was concerned. He hadn't been hurting anybody. Bear felt tears prick his eyes as he imagined Pride writhing under the whip, screaming in pain, helpless to fight back. It was enough to make Bear wish Pride's father were still alive, just so that Bear could hunt him down and do to him what he'd done to Pride.

He laid soft kisses along each scar, wishing with all his heart that his lips could erase them, wipe away the memory of Pride's pain. Pride turned in his arms then, his hands cupping Bear's cheeks, his thumbs wiping away the tears that trickled down his face.

"Don't, Bear. Done told you it was a long time ago," Pride whispered.

"I know it. Can't help it, though. It hurts when I think on how much you suffered, Pride. Wish I'd been there to keep that bastard off you."

Pride smiled sadly and kissed Bear, a long, slow, soft kiss that made Bear's whole body tingle.

Bear tossed the soap and cloth to the side, sliding his hands over the still-damp skin of Pride's hips, cupping his ass and pulling him closer, deepening the kiss. He pushed his tongue past Pride's lips, hungry now, his lust flaring as he felt Pride's erection dance with his own.

He left Pride's mouth and bent his head, suckling fiercely at Pride's throat. "What's it like?" Bear asked, whispering against Pride's tender flesh. "To be inside a man, I mean. What's it feel like?"

Pride groaned, tilting his head for Bear's lips and wrapping his arms around his waist. His hands slid across Bear's back, hugging him close enough for their cocks to dig into one another's belly. "Do you want to find out? Do you want to fuck me, Bear?" he asked.

"Yeah, I think I do, if'n you don't mind it, Pride. I want to know what's it like to be that close to you. *Inside* you," Bear moaned softly. He bit down gently on Pride's shoulder, then slowly worked his way back up Pride's neck to his mouth. Pride tasted like whiskey and a bit of the cinnamon they'd sprinkled on their flapjacks that morning, and Bear couldn't get enough as he thrust his tongue past Pride's lips, swirling it over and around

Pride's.

"You ain't small, Bear," Pride whispered, taking Bear's cock into his hand. "Gonna have to let me lead you in this, or you're like as not rip me in two."

"Okay, Pride. Whatever you say. Just hurry," Bear breathed, pushing himself into Pride's hand. "I'm so fucking hard it hurts."

He watched Pride pad across the kitchen to the cupboard, quickly returning with the jar of lard. "Sit down on the chair, Bear," he instructed, popping open the jar and scooping out a handful of thick, white grease.

Bear did as he was told, sitting down and watching Pride intently. His cock felt like a firebrand, so hard that it was painful, his balls swollen up and aching for release. When Pride wrapped his hand around his shaft and coated it with a thick layer of lard, Bear threw his head back and groaned.

Pride turned his back to Bear and bent forward a bit, reaching one hand behind himself. Two fingers, coated with grease, probed between his cheeks until they found his asshole. Watching Pride coat himself, then sink two fingers deeply inside himself nearly threw Bear over the edge. That's where his cock was going – inside of Pride's body. The thought alone was almost enough to make him come. It was only by sheer will that he kept himself from spilling as he watched Pride ready his ass for Bear's cock.

His breath caught in his throat when Pride removed his fingers and backed up, reaching for Bear's erection. As he slowly sat down on Bear's lap, impaling himself on Bear's hard cock, Bear felt his mind and body shatter into a million pieces, overwhelmed by the ecstasy washing over him.

Hot. *Good God, I'm gonna be burnt alive*, Bear thought wildly. He'd never felt anything like it in all his sorry life. Silky smooth, pulsing and squeezing and so goddamn hot that Bear feared his dick would catch fire and burn to a cinder. Deeper and deeper he slid inside Pride, until Pride's cheeks touched Bear's thighs and he was full encased in Pride's ass. Nothing could be better than this – nothing more wonderful, more breathtaking.

Then Pride began to move.

And Bear lost his mind.

Up and down, Pride slid himself over Bear's cock. He rode him slowly at first but quickly picked up speed, until he was bouncing like a demon on Bear's lap. Both men were moaning loudly, and as Pride jerked his hand over his cock, Bear grabbed his hips, helping him ride.

It became impossible for Bear to hold back. He let loose, bellowing as he came harder than he could ever remember before, emptying himself inside of Pride. Pinpoint stars flickered brightly in his vision as his muscles contracted with pleasure so intense that it bordered on pain. Reaching around Pride's hips, Bear covered Pride's hand with his own, helping him stroke his erection. Pride threw his head back and leaned against Bear's chest as their hands gave him his release.

Breathing hard, still shuddering, Bear wrapped his arms around Pride and refused to let him go. No way was he going to give this up, this feeling of connection, of being a part of Pride. No way.

They sat like that for a long while, still linked together although Bear's cock grew soft within Pride's channel. Finally, reluctantly, he allowed Pride to get up. Bear winced at the painful way Pride was walking when he went to fetch the soapy rag to clean them off.

"Damn it, Pride...I hurt you! I'm so fucking stupid – I should've never asked to go inside you. I'm too big for you. I'm sorry, Pride," Bear said, feeling his chest tighten with guilt, and a bit of panic. What if Pride was angry with him? What if he didn't want Bear to touch him anymore? What if he left? Bear couldn't even blame him if he did – not after Bear had hurt him.

"Don't you ever say that," Pride admonished, retuning with the washcloth and gently cleaning Bear's groin. "It was wonderful. *You* were wonderful. A little discomfort ain't gonna kill me. I *like* feeling you inside me, Bear," he whispered. "I like it a lot. You filled me right up, boy."

"You sure?"

"I ain't never lied to you."

"I know it. It's just that--"

"Now you just hush. I'm real tired, and we're both as clean as a pair of shiny, new whistles. What say we get some shuteye, huh?" Pride asked, leaning in and pressing his lips tenderly to Bear's.

Bear nodded, feeling a wash of relief roll over him. Pride wasn't angry. He wasn't going to leave. "Won't ask for that again, Pride. I promise."

"Don't piss me off, Bear. I just done told you that I liked you being inside me," Pride chided, looking Bear in the eye. "I *liked* it. Understand?"

A slow smile spread across Bear's face and quickly grew into a grin, as he nodded. "Then you really don't mind if once in a while..."

"Nope. Don't mind at all. As a matter of fact, I might just insist on it from time to time," Pride said, returning Bear's smile.

Crawling into bed, they wrapped themselves in one another's arms and drifted off into an exhausted, well-earned sleep, not waking until well past mid-morning of the following day.

Chapter Thirteen

A queen, prettier than a twenty-dollar whore, joined two of her sisters in Zack's hand. He was on a roll, having won four of the last five hands, a definite improvement over the rash of bad luck he'd had all winter. The heartburn that had been sizzling from his stomach to his chest all day had eased off a bit, although his face remained poker straight showing none of the relief he felt. It appeared he'd have the money to pay for his room after all. For a while he'd been sure that Frank was going to chuck him out ass first into the snow when the rent came due and Zack's pockets were empty.

He hadn't made it down into St. Elmo's before the storm hit. It had blown in from over the mountains before he'd even reached Snake Creek, the wind howling loud enough to deafen a man. The snow had fallen so fast and so thick that he'd lost his bearings a time or two, wandering off the trail into the thicker wood. If he hadn't found his way again as fast as he did, he would have died from exposure before he ever made it out of the foothills. As it was he'd lost one of his horses to the storm. Finally, hunched low over the saddle, covered head-to-foot in a thick layer of snow and frozen half to death, he'd made it to the town's stable just in time. Another few minutes and he'd have toppled from the saddle, too weak and bone-cold to move.

Within days, the bullet furrow on his arm had festered. His forearm had swelled up to twice its normal size, his wound seeping ugly yellow pus, and the only person in town available to doctor it had been the saloon's cook. With her black teeth and sour breath, it had been all Zack could do to allow her grimy fingers to touch him.

She'd stuck a dirty rag between his teeth and had sliced open Zack's skin open with kitchen knife to let the poison drain out. He'd screamed bloody hell against the foul-tasting rag, and it had taken Billy Zanders and Frank Wilcox both to hold Zack down while she'd worked on him.

While he'd been out cold, knocked senseless by the pain and half a bottle of whiskey, she'd taken two dollars from his coin purse for her troubles.

Bitch. If Zack hadn't been worried that Frank Wilcox, the barkeep and saloon owner -- and a man with a temper every bit as ornery as Zack's own -- wouldn't have shot Zack's frostbitten ass, he'd have sliced the thieving whore wide open.

He'd burned with fever for several days after. It was a miracle that Zack had survived, since no one in that miserable shit of a town gave a lick whether he did or not. He awoke with his lips dry and cracked, his bed and clothes soaked through with sweat and vomit, and a renewed resolve to kill Bear and his friend for the misery they'd caused him.

He pushed the memory away, concentrating on his hand. Upping the ante, his ice-blue eyes flicked from face to face around the table, trying to read the other men's cards in their expressions.

"Whatever happened to that Levi fella who was running

with you last summer, Zack?" Billy asked, pouring a splash of whiskey into a shot glass. He bottomed up, a thin amber trickle dripping from the corner of his mouth into his grizzled beard. "He was one mean bastard. Near as bad-tempered as you, Zack," Billy laughed, pouring himself another round. "And that young pup that was trailing after you...what's his name? Jed?"

"Jeb. He's dead. They both are."

Billy paused with his shot glass halfway to his mouth. "Dead? How?"

"Murdered."

"Goddamn. Thought you boys were headed up into the mountains to do some hunting. What happened?"

"That bastard Bear got 'em. You know the one. Been living up on the mountain by himself for years. Man's crazier than a shithouse rat. Snuck up on our camp in the middle of the night and shot 'em both dead in their sleep for no fucking good reason. I was lucky to get away with just a scratch on my arm," Zack said, keeping his expression emotionless and his eyes trained on his cards. He'd told the lie in his head so often that it was beginning to ring true to his ears and flowed easily off his tongue.

"Shit, that don't sound like Bear," Billy said, tossing back his shot.

Zack's hand left the table, inching slowly toward the holster at his hip. "You calling me a liar?"

Billy frowned, setting his glass down so hard that it rattled. "Maybe. It don't seem like something Bear would do. And if you're in a mind to reach for your gun, I promise you that you'll have a hole between your eyes before you can pull it free."

"Knock off the shit, the two of you," Frank called from the bar. Zack turned and saw that Frank had his shotgun out, leveled to his shoulder and pointed right between Zack's eyes. "Ain't gonna have none of that in here. Gonna be a long enough winter without you trying to shoot every poor sumbitch that looks at you cross-eyed, Zack."

"I ain't shot nobody," Zack growled, narrowing his eyes at Billy. "Yet."

"You ain't *gonna* shoot nobody, either. Don't even be thinking about it. You got a problem with any man in here, you can just scoot your sorry ass outside into the snow."

Zack fought to contain the fury that was roiling in his gut. These bastards were all the same. Always sticking up for each other, even for an asshole like Bear. He swallowed his gall, and placed his hand back on the table. "Ain't got no problem, Frank," he said, staring hard at Billy.

"Good. Keep it that way and I won't have to be scraping your brains off the floor."

The game played on, until Zack and Billy were the only players left. Billy threw down two pair, aces and eights, and Zack spread his three queens out with a flourish and a mean, spiteful grin. Sweeping his arm across the table, he pulled in the pile of chips from its center.

Zack's fingers played idly with the chips in front of him, letting them slide through his fingers, clacking woodenly back down onto the pile on the table. "Just for the record, let me tell you something about your friend Bear. He shot my daddy in cold blood fifteen years ago. Right on our front porch while my Mama and sister was watching. Didn't have no reason to do that, just plum craziness. Now he's gone and killed Jeb and Levi the same way, and near enough killed me. He's a sick, sorry sumbitch."

"Sorry your daddy got killed, Zack, but I never heard nothing about Bear being a wanted man."

"Him and the sheriff was *close* friends, if you know what I mean. Sheriff got himself shot by a man three months after Bear went on the run. Never caught the man, but tongues wagged that it was Bear. Jealous that the Sheriff got himself married. Now I hear tell that Bear's got a man living with him in that shack of his."

"Yeah? So what?"

"So, what's a man like Bear doing with another man holed up in that cabin all winter?"

"You're full of shit, Zack. Bear ain't like that. When he comes in for supplies he always beds down one of the girls."

"Yeah, I guess they're just playing mumblety pegs up there, huh?" Zack sniffed, pocketing his winnings as he stood up. He looked Frank in the eye. "You mark my words, Frank. Them two is up to no good. They're nothing but two bad peas in the same rotten pod, if you ask me. Somebody ought to go up there come spring and get 'em afore they murder you all in your sleep."

"Somebody like you, Zack?"

"Maybe. Be doing this town a service if'n I did."

"Don't do us any favors, Zack. What Bear does up in his cabin is his own damn business. It don't concern us. This town is peaceful, not like Dodge or Tombstone. We don't cotton to men taking the law into their own hands here. If you move against Bear, you'll most likely end up with a quick drop and a sudden stop yourself."

"Well then, it's your funeral, Frank. Don't say I didn't warn you," Zack growled. He turned away and stamped up the stairs to his room, slamming the door shut behind him.

Come spring, the Snake Creek overflowed her banks, a wall of muddy water churning down over the main street in St. Elmo's, turning it into a stinking quagmire.

It had washed away large chunks of the wooden

sidewalks that had lined the street on both sides, leaving the people no choice but to jump the gaps or wallow their way through the thick muck.

The water had flooded the first floors of most of the buildings, including the saloon, saturating the old, dried out timber floors. When the water had finally receded, it left everything reeking with a damp sour stench.

Watching the street below through the dirty, cracked glass of the window, Zack scowled, his hand fisting the fabric of the faded and grayed gingham curtains that hung across it. Behind him, his saddlebag sat on his bed, packed tight with clothing and supplies.

He'd been all set to leave, to head back into the hills and finish what he'd started last fall, when the flood had hit. Sorely tempted to leave anyway, his common sense had finally scored a hit on his impatience at the last moment. If the streets of St. Elmo's had been turned into a muddy swamp by the flood then the hills were most likely no better, and no more negotiable than they would have been in the dead of winter. It was still raining, and even though his britches burned to get a move on, Zack knew that more floods could be possible. He had no more a wish to drown in a sudden flash flood than he had had to be frozen to death.

Still, it was frustrating, and his fist pounded the top of the dresser that sat next to the window. Another few days holed up in the rat hole that passed itself off as a hotel room, and Zack might just lose his mind.

The room was tiny, no more than an overgrown closet. A single bed, a dresser, and a pitcher and basin were the only luxuries his two-bits-a-day bought him. The ragged quilt that covered the bed was moth-eaten, and the mattress, nearly thin enough to see through, stunk of piss. Faded cabbage-rose wallpaper had been peeled away in long strips in places, exposing the bare, worm-ridden wooden walls.

Sitting down on the bed, its springs creaking noisily from his weight, Zack took out a flask of whiskey from his saddlebag and tipped it back. The cheap rotgut burned his throat, but warmed his belly and soothed his nerves.

Soon. Very soon he'd be able to leave and head up into the hills. His plan was simple. Under the cover of night, he'd sneak up on Bear's cabin. Hidden in the brush, he'd wait until Bear and that skinny friend of his came outside. He'd shoot them both before they ever knew what hit them.

Bear's bugger-buddy would die first, Zack decided, but he wasn't going to die easy. Not after killing Levi and giving Zack the bullet-burn that had nearly done him in. He ran a finger over the thick, rough scar that stretched along the length of his forearm. Maybe a gut shot – let him die the way Levi had. Yes, Zack decided, that would be a fitting end for the interfering little bastard.

Bear was another story altogether. Zack was going to see to it that Bear suffered like no man ever had before. He'd die, but he'd die slowly, and only after Zack had had his fill of torturing him. Zack had waited far too long to let Bear off the hook with a quick and easy death. Then, after he'd spread out whatever pieces of Bear were left for the carrion-eaters, Zack would torch his cabin. By the time Zack was done, there wouldn't be anything left to show that Bear had ever existed. The only thing that would escape intact would be the map, and that would be safely tucked away in Zack's saddlebag.

Zack would make damn sure he was long gone before any of the bleeding hearts in town realized that Bear was dead. He sure as hell wouldn't tell them. There was no way he was going to swing for getting revenge on his pa's death.

He had no set idea of what he'd do after Bear was

dead. Most likely, he'd hunt up that treasure -- whatever it might be -- but then, well, who knew? Zack never thought beyond the moment of his revenge. It had been all he'd thought about for years, had consumed his every waking moment and most of his dreams. Killing Bear was all he lived for, and he had no plans for the rest of his life afterward.

Truth was, he really didn't care.

And that made him all the more dangerous.

Chapter Fourteen

Pride had to admit that he was a tiny bit saddle sore come morning. He eased himself onto his chair at the table, trying not to wince. The last thing he wanted was for Bear to feel badly about the night before. Bear's face, as he set down a piping hot cup of coffee in front of Pride, told Pride that he wasn't as successful as he'd hoped to be.

"Damn it, I really did hurt you last night," Bear growled, smacking his thigh with a meaty fist. "Goddamn it, Pride, you shouldn't have let me do it."

"Nah, I done slept wrong is all. Got a kink in my back. It'll work itself out soon enough, Bear," Pride answered, keeping his eyes on his coffee as he stirred in a healthy spoonful of sugar. He watched the granules dissolve into the strong black liquid, and lowered his head over the cup, breathing deep and filling his lungs with the delicious aroma. He prattled on, hoping to distract Bear – and himself – from his sore butt. "You do make a fine cup of coffee, Bear. Did I ever tell you about the coffee they served us back in Rock Island? Shit, piss water is what it was. All they did was fill a pot with water and wave the grounds at it from across the yard. 'Course, that was when they were generous enough to *give* us coffee, which wasn't damned near as often as we'd have liked. Made do most of the time with plain water."

"Bullshit. You're trying to change the subject."

"Ain't no subject to change, Bear. I done told you last night that I'm fine."

"Then why are you sitting there like that chair was the chopping block and your ass was the chicken?"

"We're running low on supplies. Gonna have to make a trip down to St. Elmo's soon," Pride said, blowing across the lip of his cup before taking a sip. Bear needed to let it go. Pride was fine – *more* than fine. He just had a bit of a hitch in his git-along at the moment. He'd live. The way Bear had made him feel the night before was worth every twinge he'd felt since.

"Shit, if you ain't a stubborn mule, and that's a fact. Yeah, we got those hides from last fall that we just finished tanning the other day. We can trade 'em for supplies down at the general store. Bart always gives me a fair dollar for them."

"What say we take a hike up into the hills today to that outcrop, Bear? Ground is dry again, and the weather looks nice."

Bear nodded, setting their breakfast plate down on the table and settling himself in. "All right. Soon as we finish breakfast we can head out. Maybe we can tote a tent and some supplies with us, spend the night out there. These walls are closing in on me lately."

Pride smacked the top of the table with his palm so hard that their cups rattled. "Now, that's the finest idea I've heard in a long time! Spend a night out under the stars; maybe do some fishing, if we have the time. Nothing like fresh fish cooked over a campfire."

"The streams up there have some fine brook trout. Got a couple of poles we can take up with us."

"Damn, son! This is turning into a regular holiday, ain't it?" Pride grinned, lifting his cup toward Bear. "Camping out, fishing, treasure-hunting, other things… "

"Other things?" Bear asked, cocking a brow at Pride.

"Don't get better than lovin' under the night sky in front of a cracklin' fire, boy. Give them forest critters a show."

Bear laughed, shaking his head. "You sure are a peculiar fella, Pride. Sweet and pretty to look at, but as peculiar as a three-headed dog."

Chuckling, Pride nodded. "Well, I might be peculiar but at least I don't bore you none."

"Now, that's true enough," Bear smiled, digging into his flapjacks with gusto. "Guess maybe I'll keep you around for a spell."

"Oh, you will, huh?"

"Yeah," Bear said, looking at Pride over his forkful of hotcakes. "You're a keeper."

There was a sudden softness in his eyes that Pride hadn't seen before, not even after sex. It sent a shiver down Pride's spine, and brought a hot stinging to the corners of his eyes.

Bear cleared his throat and shoved another tremendous forkful of food into his mouth, returning his attention to his plate.

Pride watched him for a while, silently, unable to find anything to say. He settled for reaching over the table and covering the hand that wasn't shoveling food into Bear's mouth with his own.

Pride stood atop the outcrop, holding Bear's map up in his hands. He angled it, trying to catch the rays of sunshine that filtered in through the trees. Standing next to him, Bear read the map from over Pride's shoulder.

"Bear, shove over, boy. You're blocking my light. I can't read this damn thing with your big ol' shadow hanging over me."

Grunting, Bear stepped to side, allowing a beam of light to hit the hide map. "There! See that?" Pride grinned, pointing to a black, jagged line that had been drawn on the map at its midpoint just northwest of the skull marking. "This line here has to be that ridge over yonder." He nodded toward a vertical rock ridge that rose up sharply at the base of the mountain, about a half-mile from the outcrop.

Bear nodded, taking the map from Pride. He looked from the map to the rocky wall and back again. "Looks like this tombstone mark ain't but a stone's throw from there, Pride. We can't climb it, though. It's too steep. We'd break our necks if we was to try. Gonna have to find a way around it, come up the backside of it."

"Reckon you're right. Tomorrow then. It's too late today to do much before dark besides catch us some fish and fry 'em up for supper," Pride agreed, clapping Bear on the back. "Let's go, then. I'm as hungry as a bear," he teased. He chuckled when Bear's stomach took that exact moment to rumble loudly.

"Yeah," Bear laughed, "Me, too, I guess."

"You? You're always hungry."

"Well, I'm a big man, ain't I?"

"That you are, my friend. *All* over," Pride grinned.

Bear grimaced. "You ain't still hurting, are you?"

"Nope. Not a bit. Matter of fact, I'm about ready for more of the same. Been toting wood for the better part of the afternoon."

"So I noticed."

"Now, Bear, how would you know that if you wasn't looking?" Pride grinned, shouldering Bear as they walked back toward their camp.

"Didn't have to look. You been shoving that thing at me every chance you got today. Pretty damn hard to miss it when it's poking at your ass or your hip every five minutes."

"Sorry, Bear. It's got a mind of its own. Don't behave itself worth a lick where you're concerned."

Bear laughed, shaking his head as he shouldered their fishing poles. "Well, you best teach it some manners. You let it out of your britches while we're fishing and the trout might mistake it for bait."

"Oh, now that was just hurtful, Bear," Pride said, looking wounded. He held his hound dog expression for nearly thirty seconds before he broke and laughed along with Bear.

The hike to the stream was a short, easy one. Sitting down on the mossy bank, the two men relaxed. They fitted their fishing poles, two thin, yellowish-green willow switches that Bear had trimmed and smoothed, with lines of string. Baiting the lines, they cast them into the crystal clear, babbling water.

"This here crick reminds me of one that ran across the back acres of our land when I was a boy," Bear said. "My brothers and me caught a wagonload of fish in that stream when we was young. Used to bring 'em home and clean 'em ourselves, so that Ma only had to throw 'em in batter and fry 'em up. Ma sure loved fish, but she hated cleaning the damn things."

Pride looked over at Bear, and felt his heart clench at the melancholy that shadowed his features. It was plain that thinking on his family still hurt, even after all the time that had passed. He was well acquainted with the feeling, although while Bear felt sad when he thought of his family, Pride felt empty and hateful. Patting his arm, Pride tried to take Bear's mind off his memories. "When I was a boy, my grandpa taught me how to noodle fish.

You ever done that, Bear?"

"No. What is it?"

"Fishing without a pole," Pride said, grinning at Bear's look of disbelief. "I'll see if I can show you what I mean. Don't work all the time, so don't get your hopes up. You just set still and don't move that line of yours." He quickly stripped off his boots and socks, and rolled his pants up to his knees. Wading out into the cold, knee-deep stream, Pride bent over and let his hands dangle in under the surface, standing perfectly still. The only things that moved were his eyes as they scanned the crystal clear water and rocky bottom for movement. After several minutes, his patience was rewarded.

A dark shape slithered toward him, and moving as quickly as greased lightning, he swept his hands through the water. In one smooth movement, he flipped the fish out of the water onto the bank. He laughed out loud at the look of surprise on Bear's face when a goodish sized trout nearly landed in his lap, flopping crazily in the dirt.

"How'd you do that?" Bear asked incredulously as the fish finally stopped thrashing and lay still.

"Takes practice and patience. And like I said, it don't always work. Most times they get away. I was just lucky today to get one on the first try."

"Hey, I got a bite!" Bear grinned, watching his line bob in the water. A few moments later he hauled a second, larger fish onto the bank.

"Well now, ain't she a beauty? I reckon we're gonna stuff ourselves tonight and still have some leftover for breakfast," Pride laughed. He strung the two fish together as Bear gathered their poles. Carrying the fish and his shoes and socks, he followed Bear back to their campsite.

Pride set about kindling the fire while Bear cleaned the fish. In short order the fish were frying over the fire, sizzling and smelling better and better by the minute, making their stomachs rumble loudly, reminding them both of how hungry they were.

They ate the trout straight out of the frying pan, along with a mason jar of put-up beans that Bear had brought with them. Afterwards, they lay on their backs, sipping whiskey from Bear's flask, silently watching the stars wink on in between the gaps in the treetops.

There was no need to fill the air between them with conversation. The silence wasn't strained or tense; it was soothing, like a favorite old shirt that had grown soft and comfortable over time. The silence fit them perfectly.

And when Bear rolled over on top of Pride, his lips and hands seeking contact with Pride's flesh, Pride eagerly gave over to him. He sighed as Bear's lips traced a path of fire down over his chest; moaned as he rocked himself up into Bear's calloused but gentle hands. In turn, Bear's breathy noises joined Pride's, their voices becoming one and blending with the quiet sounds of the night.

There was still no need for words. Each knew the other so well that he knew exactly where to stroke, where to touch, where to lick to send the other soaring without needing to ask or tell. There was no need to link their bodies to feel the connection between them, not this time. When they came, their release was as hushed as the rest of sounds of nature around them -- sweet and soft, satisfying and peaceful.

Dawn found them breaking camp, eager to be on their way. The hike up and around the ridge took longer than either of them had anticipated, and it was early afternoon before they crested the top of the rise.

They made camp there, pitching their tent at the back of the windswept rock where the trees offered some protection from the elements. Behind the tree line rose the great craggy peaks of the Rockies, so high that they wore bonnets of snow all year round. Painted in shades of blue and white, the sheer size of the mountains made a man feel as puny as an ant crawling over the forest floor. Pride wondered how anyone could have taken it into their heads to climb the damn things in the first place. How could a man think to stand against such power and win?

He shook his head, returning his attention to the map Bear held in his hands.

"Well, we're on the ridge. If we're right, then the tombstone mark and the 'X' should be somewhere right over there," Bear said, pointing toward the northwest. "Don't look like it's too far, neither, maybe a quarter mile or so."

Pride grinned up at Bear, slapping him on the back. "Well, what are we waiting for? Let's go, boy!" He trotted over to the tent and rummaged through the small pile of tools they'd lugged along with them. Retrieving a short-handled pickaxe and a shovel, he shouldered the axe and handed the shovel to Bear.

"What are you going to buy with the treasure, Bear?" Pride asked as they made their way northwest.

"There ain't nothing saying that there even *is* a treasure, Pride. You're getting your hopes up, now."

Pride rolled his eyes and huffed. "Supposing that there *is* one, Bear. What are you going to buy with all that money?"

Bear shifted the shovel from one shoulder to the other. "I don't know. Never really thought about it afore. Only thought as far as finding it, not what I would do with it once it was found. A new Bowie knife to replace the one I lost, I guess."

"A knife? You find yourself a treasure and all you're

going to buy is a *knife*?" Pride laughed, shaking his head. "Lord, Bear, somebody has got to teach you how to dream big."

"That so? Well, Mr. Big Dreams, what are you going to buy with your half?" Bear asked.

"*My* half? It ain't my treasure, Bear. It's yours. You're the one that owns the map. You're the one that's been searching for it for all these years. I'm just along for the company."

Bear scowled down at Pride. "No, you ain't. If we find this thing then you get half of whatever it is. Now don't start squabbling with me, Pride," he continued, putting out a palm to discourage the argument that was already dancing on Pride's tongue. "That's just the way it's going to be. My mind's made up on it."

Pride paused, feeling his throat burn with a sudden rush of emotion. "You'd do that? Give away half your treasure to a stranger? You ain't got no idea of how much there might be, Bear. You might be giving away millions!"

"And I might be giving away two-bits or less. Like you said, there's no telling how much it might be worth, or even if there is a treasure at all. Besides, you ain't a stranger."

"I ain't your kinfolk, neither."

"Feels like it. As far as I'm concerned, you're family, Pride. The only family I've had in a long, long time. What's mine is yours, and I don't want to hear another dang word about it."

Pride felt his eyes burn and rubbed his sleeve across them. "Damn wind. Blowing dust in my eyes," he lied. After a moment or two, he said quietly, "You too, I reckon."

Bear cleared his throat, staring down at his feet as they walked along silently for a few moments, then asked, "So, what are you gonna buy?"

"Me? I'm gonna buy you the biggest, shiniest Bowie knife west of the Mississippi, that's what. One that's got a solid ivory handle and fancy engraving. And a fine sheath for it, too. The best I can find."

"I can buy my own Bowie. What are you going to buy for *you*, Pride?"

"Stubborn goat," Pride grinned, as he swung the pickaxe to his other shoulder. Damn thing was heavy, and his shoulder was beginning to ache from carrying it. He could use a rest, but he was more eager to get on with the search.

"Now, why would you want to buy a *stubborn* goat? Seems to me that if I had my choice, I'd pick a sociable one instead." Bear grinned, lowering the shovel and leaning on the handle.

Pride snorted, relenting and setting the head of the pickaxe down on the ground, looking up at Bear. "I don't reckon I know what I'd buy. Clothes maybe. Replace my rifle that those varmints stole from me. Maybe buy a horse or two. We could build a stable up by the cabin for them. And I always wanted to see the ocean. We could take us a trip out west, Bear. Sleep in swanky hotels and eat fancy grub, like the rich folk in Denver."

"Ain't much for putting on airs, myself, but traveling some sounds like a fine idea, Pride. Never been over the mountains."

"Well, we ain't going anywhere standing here jawing. Got to find us the treasure afore we can buy anything. Keep your eyeballs peeled. If that map is right, then that tombstone mark should be somewhere around here, Bear," Pride said, scanning the vegetation around them. "Maybe we should split up. You head over there," Pride said, pointing to the north, "And I'll scout around to the west. Cover more ground that way."

Bear nodded, moving off through the thick underbrush.

Pride continued moving slowly through the trees, heading in a general westerly direction. There didn't seem to be anything that looked like a tombstone anywhere. All he saw were countless junipers and cedars, and a thick carpet of yarrow, dandelions, wild onion, and scattered patches of white mushrooms. Taking a break, he lowered the head of the pickaxe to the ground. Leaning back against the rough bark of a tree, he admired the scenery.

Sure was pretty up here, Pride admitted as he looked around. So different from the dust-choked prairies he'd been raised on. There, the only colors had been dun, brown, and gold. Here, there was every shade of the rainbow – the blue of the mountain peaks, the deep green of the forest, the reds, whites, and yellows of the wildflowers underfoot. Sweet, clean air, and more food-on-the-hoof than a body could ever need. There was plenty of wood for building, and plenty of land for building on. Made a man wonder why anyone would choose to live anywhere else.

Of course, surviving in God's Country took a lot of effort and not a little luck. Pride had seen that for himself over the past winter. The bitter cold, the snow, the spring floods – it wasn't an easy life, and that's a fact. Pride wondered whether he would have been able to survive it as well as Bear had. He doubted it. Bear was a strong man, inside and out. Still, Pride felt at home here, more than he ever had anywhere he'd lived before. He'd take the hardships of living in the mountains any day, as long as Bear was the one helping him through them.

Never knew a man to grow on him like Bear had, and it wasn't just his body, neither, although Pride would be the last one to complain about the sex. It was more than that. It was more like they knew each other as well as they knew themselves. Better, maybe. Knew what the other wanted or needed without having to ask.

Lost in his thoughts, he'd just bent to pick up the axe again when Bear's voice called to him, echoing through the wood.

"Pride! Over here! I think I found something!"

Chapter Fifteen

Creeping slowly through the brush, Zack bent low, keeping himself hidden behind the screen of foliage. He placed each foot down carefully, mindful not to snap a twig and give his position away. He hadn't come this far to fail because of catching a bad case of stupid.

He'd left his horse a ways back, safely tethered to a bush. No sense in taking a chance on losing another horse – especially since he didn't have the funds to buy himself another. The extra time he'd had to spend in St. Elmo's had cost him his last two bits.

He'd been on the move for two days, without stopping to eat or sleep. His eyes were red-rimmed and dry, and his body was bone-tired, but Zack wasn't about to slow down for anything as trivial as eating or sleeping. Not now. Not when the time for his revenge that he'd so patiently waited for was finally at hand. Not when Bear was so close Zack could practically see his short hairs.

He'd had to wait longer to leave St. Elmo's than he'd expected or wanted. Snake Creek had taken her sweet ass time settling down after the last of the spring floods, and since it would have been foolish to try to cross her while she was still bloated and overflowing her banks, he'd been forced to cool his heels at the hotel. Drowning in the murky, frigid waters was not a part of Zack's plans. He might have been a lot of things, but stupid wasn't one of them.

But the wait had cost him.

Not that it was Zack's fault. A man couldn't be expected to pass long days and nights sitting on his ass, twiddling his thumbs in a piss-drenched hotel room. A man like Zack had *needs*.

Needs like whiskey, women, and gambling. Never one to deny himself anything he wanted, indulging in the three had soaked up Zack's meager funds faster than a desert sucks up rainwater. He'd finally left in the thick of the night, without paying for the last three weeks of his room and board, or for the whore he'd last bedded.

She was the reason he couldn't go back to St. Elmo's, even if he *wanted* to pay back what he owed Frank for his hotel bill. Not that he'd ever had any intention of paying up, but now he didn't have a choice in the matter. If he returned, the only way he'd leave St. Elmo's again was at the end of a rope.

It was the whore's fault. If she hadn't been so fucking demanding, so *shrill* about getting paid – with money that Zack didn't have -- then Zack wouldn't have had to hit her to shut her up. If she'd just kept her yap closed like he'd told her, he wouldn't have had to keep hitting her until he'd made sure she'd never whine at anyone ever again. Anybody with a lick of sense could see that it was her fault she was dead.

Besides, a body would think that she would have been grateful he'd even *looked* at her, let alone fucked her. Scrawny, gap-toothed bitch that she was, she should have been paying *Zack*, not the other way around.

Unfortunately, Zack knew that Frank wouldn't see it

that way. He just *knew* that the goddamn asshole would blame Zack for killing one of his whores. Which was why Zack had stuffed her body under the bed, washed off the blood as best he could, and had snuck out during the middle of the night.

But that was in the past, and neither here nor there. All that mattered now was Zack's revenge, and it was so close that Zack could taste the sweetness of it on his tongue.

Right before him, on a rise beyond the wide clearing that stretched away from where he sat hunkered down in the bush, stood a log cabin that Zack would bet his soul belonged to Bear. Only Bear was stupid enough to build a shanty all the way up here in the middle of God's hairy ass where he'd only have the deer and wolves for company.

Deer, wolves, and that interfering little bastard Bear had freed and taken under his wing. Lord knew what those two were doing up here in no man's land, where there wasn't a woman around for fifty miles. Zack didn't like to go more than a week without getting laid, and he'd bet his last dollar that a big man like Bear didn't either. Which only meant one thing, as far as Zack was concerned. Them two were buggering each other.

And that was just another reason for Zack to kill them both. Wasn't right for them to be doing that. It was unnatural. Zack knew of men who'd been hung for it. Hell, he'd helped hang a few from time to time himself.

He settled himself behind a large juniper bush, peeking through the budding foliage, focusing his attention on the cabin.

Zack's body tingled with excitement, and his fingers danced over the butts of his guns eagerly. Lord knew he'd waited long enough for this moment. Fifteen years, to be exact. He had to force himself to be cautious and not dash across the clearing, guns blazing.

There was no movement that he could see in the cabin, no signs of life. No smoke drifted from the stovepipe chimney, no sounds reached his ears.

But Zack reminded himself that it was still very early in the morning. The sun had barely crested the horizon, weak and distant, doing little to dispel the chill of the night. No wonder he couldn't spot any movement inside the cabin. They were probably both still sound asleep.

Zack grinned. They were never going to know what hit them.

Keeping his body in a crouch, he drew his guns and scooted silently across the clearing toward the cabin. Reaching the door he paused a moment, then kicked it wide open and rushed inside, ready – *itching* in fact -- to shoot the first thing that moved.

There was no one in the main room, and the hearth was cold and gray with old ashes. Spying the bed in the small alcove, he aimed the barrels of his guns at it, his fingers twitching on the triggers as he moved quickly to stand by the bed, screaming for Bear to wake up and see the face of the man who was going to kill him.

No way was Zack going to shoot Bear in his sleep. He wanted to see the fear in Bear's eyes as he died.

The bed was empty.

Zack twisted around as his eyes scanned over every inch of the room. There was no denying it. Bear and his friend were gone.

No, it couldn't be! He couldn't have missed Bear again. Not again!

His howl of fury rang in the room and in his own ears as his temper, barely kept leashed from the moment he'd left the bushes, exploded. He emptied both of his guns into Bear's bed, drilling holes into the goose down mattress and pillows. Before the final shot had caused the last of the pillows to split open in a flurry of white feathers, he'd holstered his still-smoking guns and turned away.

Mindlessly he tore through the cabin, smashing everything he could lay his hands on. In his mind, it was Bear he was destroying.

He pulled open Bear's dresser drawers, ripping and shredding what little clothing had been neatly folded within them, flinging the empty drawers to the floor.

Bursting into the main room, he threw the cupboard down to the floor, spraying the room with glass shrapnel as the mason jars that had lined the shelves shattered.

"Where'd you go, you bastard?" he screamed, flinging the tin coffee pot so hard against the wall that it dented before clattering to the floor. "Where?"

Zack's arm swept each of the shelves clear, then ground Bear's carefully whittled sculptures under his boot heel in a frenzied two-step until nothing was left but splintered fragments.

Picking up a chair, he smashed it onto the table, destroying the chair and cracking the tabletop in half, sending the wooden checkers that had been piled in neat stacks rolling across the floor. The other chair followed, raised and brought down again and again until he had nothing left but a pile of useless kindling.

Exhausted, Zack slumped to the floor surrounded by the carnage he'd created, his breathing ragged. His entire body trembled with rage, his eyes burning with tears of frustration. It wasn't fair. It just wasn't fair. Bear should have been here. But somehow that rank bastard had slipped away from Zack *again*.

For a moment, Zack contemplated torching the cabin. Burn it down to cinders, until there was nothing left but a pile of stinking ashes. He wondered if there were any matches on the mantle. It pleased him to think that he could burn down Bear's home with Bear's own matches. He'd already smashed the lanterns and lamp oil had pooled over the plank floor. It would go up easy.

Zack's eyes roamed to the mantle, then slowly drifted over the rest of the destruction he'd caused. It occurred to him then that the cabin hadn't looked deserted when he'd first burst in through the door. There had been foodstuffs still on the cupboard shelves before he'd toppled it. Mason jars full of put-ups from last season. No one would have left good food behind if they were leaving and not coming back. Clothes had been folded in the dresser, and a patchwork quilt had covered the bed. Who left behind perfectly good clothing and a warm quilt? No one would, that's who.

Bear was coming back.

Could be that they'd only gone out hunting.

Of course! That was it. They'd gone hunting overnight. Come this evening or maybe tomorrow at the latest, they'd be back, and Zack would be waiting for them. What a nasty surprise for them he'd make, too.

He crawled into a corner of the main room near the hearth, careful not to cut himself on the shards of broken glass that littered the floor. Crossing his legs Indian-style and leaning back against the wall, he settled in to wait. As he reloaded his guns with spare bullets from his coat pocket, his bared teeth in a parody of a grin, his eyes shining with madness.

Chapter Sixteen

Pride ran, threading his way in between the trees heading toward the sound of Bear's voice. He spotted Bear in a clearing, on a small plateau that had been carved into the hillside. He was bent over, inspecting something that lay at the foot of a pair of gnarled and twisted junipers. Skidding to a stop next to him, Pride looked down, panting and out of breath from his run through the forest.

"Well, I'll be goddamned," Pride whispered, looking up at Bear with wide eyes. "Think this is it?"

At their feet, nearly invisible among the leaves of the skunk cabbage that covered the roots of the two trees in a curling, green blanket, sat a small, chipped and pitted white stone marker shaped like a cross. Tipped onto its side, the marker's crossbeams formed a lopsided 'X'.

"Think somebody's buried up here?" Bear asked, swiping his coonskin hat off of his head. "Don't want to disrespect someone's final resting place. That just wouldn't be right, Pride."

"This stone ain't marked with any names, Bear. Don't most folk put the names of the dead on the stones that mark their graves?" Pride asked, hunkering down and tracing his fingers over the cold surface of the marker.

"Most times, if they can, I suppose. Maybe whoever buried this poor soul didn't have the time to carve his name in it."

"Maybe. Or maybe it ain't a body that's buried here, Bear. And if it is, we can always rebury the poor bastard. Only one way to find out," he said, taking the shovel from Bear. He touched the spaded head to the earth and placed his foot atop the metal scoop. Pride paused, looking up at Bear with a questioning look.

Bear frowned for a moment then nodded. Pride took a deep breath, then stepped down hard on the head of the shovel, forcing it to bite deeply into the soft earth.

Slowly, one shovelful at a time, Pride began to dig a square hole in the dirt that lay before the marker. He uprooted the skunk cabbage, tossing it and the rich dark soil into a growing mound to the side. He was sweating by the time the hole was a couple of feet deep and his shovel clanked against something hard.

Tossing the shovel to the side, Pride and Bear knelt down on either side of the hole, staring nervously into it as if they half expected something ugly to jump up and bite them both. When nothing did, Pride began to sweep the dirt away with his hands.

He exposed the corner of a small, simple wooden box, poking up through the dirt like a brown skeletal finger.

"Bear?" Pride asked softly, flicking his eyes up toward him. "Think it's a coffin?"

"Nah, too small for that. Unless it's... "

"Oh, Lordy, not a child..." Pride breathed, looking back down at the box he'd unearthed. "What do you want to do, Bear? It's your map, your decision to make."

Bear sat back on his heels, and Pride could see him thinking hard on it. His eyes closed, and he bit his lower lip, his throat muscles working as if he had a lump in his throat he was trying to swallow. "If it's a body, then we're gonna bury it proper. Nobody deserves to be shoved into the earth with no name on their marker, forgotten like this."

Pride nodded, reaching out and placing a hand on Bear's arm. He knew Bear was thinking of his baby sister, shot to death in her cradle all those years ago. Pride wondered who'd buried her and where, and realized that Bear had probably been tortured by that very question over the years.

Carefully, they worked to extract the box from its earthy prison. Slowly working it free from the ground, they heaved the heavy wooden crate up and settled it on the ground next to the hole.

"Sure is heavy for a coffin," Pride remarked as he stood and dusted the dirt from his hands. He crossed over the hole and hunkered down on the opposite side of the box from where Bear knelt.

The crate was roughly three feet long and two feet wide, fashioned from plain pine. Flat-headed nails had been hammered along the lid's edges, a few bent and driven in crooked.

The wood was old and soft, rotted from its years in the ground. It didn't take much effort for Bear to pry the lid free, cracking it open.

Their eyes met over the box as Bear's hand paused for a moment, then nodded slightly at each other as if coming to a mutual decision. In the next moment the muscles in Bear's arm flexed as he ripped the lid off and tossed it to the side.

A musty odor of damp earth and mold wafted up. Sitting on a blue saddle blanket was a skull. Smooth and grayish white, green with mold in places, the skull was fleshless and its empty, black eye sockets seemed to look up at Bear and Pride as if angry at them for disturbing its rest.

Least ways, that's what Pride thought for a moment. Shaking his head free of his squeamish thoughts, he looked over at Bear. "Too big for a child, Bear," he said softly. He pointed to a small bullet hole in the side of the skull. "Looks like he didn't die a natural death, either."

Bear grunted, reaching down and touching a finger to a small, neatly folded piece of parchment that sat wedged underneath the skull. He bit his lip as he carefully slid it out, bringing it up into the light of day for the first time since it had been buried.

Unfolding it, mindful of the crackling of the delicate parchment and the crumbling bits that fell as it opened, Bear angled it so that he could read the black scrawl that covered it.

"*Weathers Smith and me was partners. But he done wanted more than his share, and tried to kill me to git it. I kilt him first, and buried his haid with his rightful share, left the rest of the sumbitch for the wolves. Signed this year of the Lord, 1802, Bill Hicks.*"

"Been in the ground near to seventy years, Bear," Pride whispered, touching a finger to the bullet hole that pierced the skull. "Long afore either of us was born."

"Yeah."

"Think we should just stick him back in the ground and forget it?"

"What do you think, Pride?"

"Me? I think a thief don't deserve to spend eternity with the treasure he tried to kill his partner over, that's what I think," Pride said, frowning down at the skull. "'Sides, it ain't doing him no good now, anyway. I think he's way past spending it."

Bear chuckled. "Guess you're right about that. Still and all, we'll bury Mr. Smith right and proper after."

"All right, Bear." Pride gently lifted the skull from the

blanket, setting it to the side. "Go on now, Bear. It was your map that brought us here. You do the honors," he said, gesturing toward the saddle blanket.

Bear picked up a corner of the blanket between his fingers, then looked at Pride one more time. In one smooth movement, he whisked the dusty, stiff blanket out of the box.

Underneath lay hundreds of small, lumpy stones, most a pale yellow color. Picking one of the rocks up, Pride weighed it in the palm of his hand. "Lord, Bear! Do you think that this is... "

"Gold?" Bear finished for him, taking another misshapen lump from the box. He held it up into the light, turning it this way and that way. "Could be fool's gold, Pride. Lots of that around."

"Don't think nobody would shoot a man in the head and bury him atop a boxful of fool's gold, do you?" Pride said. He took out a small knife from his pocket, one that he'd taken from Bear's kitchen, and scraped it along the surface of the stone he held in his hand. It cut a groove in the malleable material of the rock. "Soft like gold, Bear. Fool's gold don't cut like this."

"Shit," Bear breathed, looking from the gold ingot in his hand to the hundreds more that lay in the box. "There must be a fortune here, Pride."

A slow, broad grin creased Pride's cheeks. "Guess this will show a thing or two to all them folks that laughed at your daddy over that map, huh? Hot damn, Bear! We're rich, son!" He jumped up to his feet, dancing a jig in a small circle while Bear watched him and laughed.

"Guess so. Guess you can buy yourself the fanciest duds in Denver with your share."

"Guess you can buy yourself the shiniest, flashiest Bowie knife, huh?"

"Reckon so, and with plenty left over, too," Bear

smiled. "Well, let's get this poor fella buried in a fitting grave. What's his name?" Bear said, tossing the ingot back into the box and picking up the parchment. "Weathers Smith. Well, Mr. Weathers Smith, we surely do thank you for sharing your treasure with us, even if you didn't have much of a say so in it." He stood up and walked over to the white stone cross that had marked the grave, yanking it out of the soft earth.

"Hand me that knife of yours, Pride," he said, sitting down and resting the marker on his lap.

Pride sat down and watched respectfully as Bear crudely carved the name *Weathers Smith* and the year *1802* into the white stone. It wasn't too deep or too fancy, but it was better than the poor soul had before. He stuck the cross upright into the ground at the head of the grave.

Wrapping the skull up in the gray saddle blanket, Pride lowered it into the hole. Shoveling the dirt back into it, he watched it disappear under the rich, black soil.

"Ashes to ashes, dust to dust," Bear said solemnly, as Pride finished filling the grave and tamped the earth down with the backside of the shovel. "Dust thou art, and unto dust thou shalt return."

"Ashes to ashes, dust to dust, if God won't have him, the Devil must," Pride added with a small grin.

"Pride! It ain't right or fitting to be fooling around at a time like this," Bear chided. But the twinkle in Bear's eyes told Pride that he wasn't nearly as sore as he tried to sound. He cleared his throat then said, "Don't you mind Pride, Mr. Smith. He ain't quite right in the head sometimes. Now, you go on and rest in peace."

Pride stifled a laugh, then looked down at the box that lay open at their feet. "So, how are we going to lug this back to the cabin?" he asked, toeing a corner of the box. "It must weigh as much as I do, Bear."

"Well, then it's a good thing you ain't more than a

scrawny piece of nothing, ain't it," Bear grinned. He tossed the pickaxe to Pride, squatting down next to the box. The next thing Pride knew, Bear had shouldered the box and was starting to walk back the way they'd come.

"Bear! You can't carry that all the way back home! You'll break something."

"Ain't gonna break nothing. It ain't that heavy," Bear called back over his shoulder.

Pride knew better. Gold was heavy, and that box was chock full of it. "I don't want you to hurt yourself, Bear." Truthfully, Pride was impressed again by Bear's strength, and wondered once more how a man could be as strong as he was and yet as gentle as Pride knew him to be. "We need all your parts to be in working order."

Bear faltered, then burst out laughing as he plodded on. "I'll try my best not to hurt any good parts, Pride. Lord, but I never met a man with such a one track mind."

"You're complaining?" Pride said, trotting up to walk beside Bear. "I've grown overly fond of some of those parts, Bear." He resisted the urge to reach over and pinch Bear's backside just to prove his point. He would have too, if he hadn't been afraid that he'd make Bear drop the box. Satisfying himself with a silent promise to cup and tweak every part of Bear he had a mind to when they reached their camp, he moved ahead of Bear, pushing aside tree limbs and brambles that might trip Bear up or snag on the crate.

Chapter Seventeen

The sun had already begun its descent by the time they reached the ridge where they'd made camp and Bear wearily set the pine box down. He swept an arm across his forehead, wiping off the beads of sweat that had been dripping down into his eyes, the salt burning like the fires of Hades.

Pride was scampering around the campsite, kindling a fire and rummaging through the sack that held their supplies. In short order he had a fire crackling with a soup pot of water suspended over it, and was dicing up chunks of meat and vegetables to put into it. A long pine needle stuck out of the corner of his mouth as he chewed it for its tangy flavor.

Bear lowered himself down to the ground a ways from the fire, still too overheated from lugging the crate all the way back to sit too close. His back and shoulders were aching from the weight of the box, although he'd never admit to it. He tried to subtly stretch and work out the kinks without Pride taking notice.

It didn't work.

"You done went and hurt yourself, didn't you?" Pride chided, clucking his tongue and kneeling down behind

Bear. "Lord, you are the most stubborn man God ever placed on this earth. I done told you a million times to let me tote that crate for a while. Now look at you! Your muscles are drawn up tighter than a pair of balls in a snow bank, Bear."

"I'm fine."

"No you ain't. Don't you go and lie to me, Bear. I got eyes. I can see you're in pain," Pride said. He knelt behind Bear, taking hold of his shoulders and slowly massaging the muscles with strong, but gentle fingers. Soon enough, he slapped Bear lightly against the back of the head. "Take off this shirt, you old fool. I brought some liniment with us. Good thing too. If I didn't, you'd be stiffer than a board come morning."

"You worry more than an old woman, Pride."

"Yeah? Well, I need to, since you're more mulish than an old man."

Bear huffed in disagreement, but shrugged out of his shirt and long johns, shivering as the cool air hit his work-warmed body. He sighed deeply as Pride's fingers began to work the pungent liniment into his skin.

"Lordy, but that stuff stinks worse than a bull's backside."

"Been sniffing bulls' backsides lately, have you?" Pride laughed, and Bear grunted as Pride's thumbs worked at a particularly sensitive knot under his left shoulder blade.

"Only one backside I'm interested in sniffing," Bear grinned, looking up over his shoulder at Pride. "And touching, and licking... "

Pride snorted, spitting the pine needle out to the side. "And you got the nerve to tell me that *I* have a one-track mind? If I didn't know any better, I'd say you was fixing to start something here, Bear."

"What if I am?"

"Then you'd best start it and finish it afore that stew is

ready, or else it'll burn while you're doing all that sniffing, touching, and licking."

Bear laughed, then turned and caught Pride around the waist and, ignoring the painful protests of his back, dragged Pride around and onto his lap. Laying him down, Bear stretched out, covering Pride's body with his own and kissed him hard and hungry. His cock twitched against Pride's belly, eager to be set free.

What was it about this man that lit Bear's groin up like a bonfire every damned time he touched him? Hell, every damn time he *looked* at him? Already his dick was stiffening, pushing at the soft fabric of his pants, straining at the buttoned fly, and all Bear had done was touch his lips to Pride's. But those lips, as always, had made Bear feel soft and mushy inside even as his cock grew painfully hard. He rocked his hips against Pride's belly, wanting him to feel how his kisses were affecting him.

Naked from the waist up, Bear's skin rubbed against the coarse fabric of Pride's shirt. It wasn't enough, not by a long shot. Bear needed to feel skin next to his, to feel Pride's nipples harden and press up tight against his chest. He sat up only long enough to roughly unbutton Pride's shirt and underwear, yanking the shirttails free from Pride's pants. Peeling the shirts open, Bear rubbed his hand slowly across the smooth expanse of Pride's chest, pausing to rub a calloused thumb across Pride's rosy nipples.

Growling, he took Pride's mouth again with sloppy openmouthed kisses that grew deeper and more demanding as his cock rubbed against Pride's thigh. Pride moaned and wriggled beneath him, his hands everywhere, kneading Bear's shoulders, his chest, tickling at his stomach until they closed over Bear's cock, squeezing it through the fabric of his pants.

Abruptly Bear sat up, breathing hard and fumbling

with the fly of his pants. "Get them trousers down now, boy, else I'll be fixing to tear 'em off you. Unless you want to hike home through the woods as naked as the day you was born, you'd better get a move on," he hissed through clenched teeth, as he jerked open his pants and lifted his bottom, sliding them down to his ankles. "'Cause I promise you there won't be nothing left but rags if you don't move quick enough."

Pride gaped at him, but hustled to pull his pants down to his knees. His cock sprang free, hard and glistening, and Pride wrapped his fingers around its length, a teasing smile playing at his lips. "Fast enough for you?" he asked, the smile widening into a grin. "Now look at what I let loose. What are you going to do about this, boy?"

"What do you want me to do about it?" Bear's voice was gruff, edgy with his own deepening need.

"Put your mouth on it. I want to feel--"

Bear didn't give Pride the chance to finish his sentence. He dove for Pride's cock, capturing it eagerly between his lips like he was a drunkard and Pride the last drop of whiskey on earth, his hand roughly knocking Pride's away. Pride's shaft burned under his hand like a hot coal, while his tongue tasted drops of liquid heat, salty and tangy. He drew in the full length of it, holding it in his mouth for a few heartbeats before letting it slide slowly out again.

Pride's fingers twisted in his hair, pushing Bear's head down over his cock, and as strong as Bear was, he couldn't find the strength or the will to resist. He allowed Pride to control the speed and the depth, taking him in fully until his nose brushed against Pride's crisp pubic hair.

His own cock was left pitifully unattended, weeping with frustration, until finally Bear could stand no more. He let Pride's cock slide from between his lips with an audible *pop* then, ignoring Pride's disappointed grunt, heaved his body up and over Pride's. Straddling his lean hips, he leaned down, supporting his weight on his elbows, his tangle of dark hair falling forward to brush Pride's cheeks. Slowly, he began to rock his hips, rubbing their cocks against one another.

This was paradise. Heaven right here on earth, lying flushed and panting beneath him. Bear found it in Pride's whipcord body and deep brown eyes. It was in the fingers that dug into Bear's biceps, and in the soft, warm breath that smelled of whiskey and pine. It was in the searing heat and velvet skin of his erection and the sweet friction it was making against Bear's. Mostly, Bear found it in the way Pride made him feel, like Bear was the only man on earth worth knowing and loving. The way Pride made Bear feel special. Needed. Wanted.

Bear rumbled deep in his chest as he ground his shaft against Pride's, leaning down and capturing his lips again, loving the feel of Pride's scratchy whiskers against his cheek and the softness of his tongue. Lordy, but Pride could melt Bear's heart with a single look, and sizzle his innards with one touch. Hell, just the *thought* of his body sliding up tight next to Bear's skin was enough to set his britches on fire. How could one man -- one scrawny, sunbrowned, *tetchy* man at that – turn another man's world on its ear so easily? Just with a word, or a look? Just by being alive?

Pride did that to him. *His* Pride. Tossed his entire life topsy-turvy, and Bear was glad of it. Bear realized in that moment that he'd never be the same after knowing Pride, after loving him. If Pride ever left him he'd leave behind a hole too deep and wide for anyone else to ever fill.

A powerful feeling of possessiveness and sudden fear swept through Bear like a flash flood and he slipped his arms under Pride, rolling onto his back and pulling Pride up on top of his chest. Trapped between them, their cocks pulsed with need, wet, hot, and aching as both of them hovered at the edge.

"Tell me you ain't gonna leave me, Pride. Tell me you're going to stay. Promise me," Bear pleaded, shocked at the panicked tone in his voice. He'd never begged for anything before in his entire life. If he couldn't get it on his own, he simply did without it. But for Pride he'd beg on his hands and knees if that was what it took.

"I ain't going anywhere, Bear," Pride whispered, ducking down and kissing Bear hard as he ground his pelvis against Bear's stomach. "Can't. My home's with you now, and I ain't *never* leaving home again."

His promise was all the catalyst needed to send Bear soaring with the eagles. Crying out as he came, Pride's words echoing in his ears, his arms crushing Pride to his chest, Bear filled the space between them with liquid heat. Pride followed him only a heartbeat or two later, groaning Bear's name through gritted teeth as his body shuddered.

"You meant what you said just now?" Bear asked quietly, rubbing Pride's back. Pride's breath was warm against his neck, the slick between their bellies cooling. There were rocks digging into Bear's back, his muscles were sore and stiff from carrying the gold, his feet ached, and he was starting to feel the cold against his sweated skin, and yet he was more at peace, more comfortable than he could ever recall being before and felt no inclination to move.

"'Course I meant it. I said it, didn't I?"

"Lots of people say things they don't mean. Make promises they don't mean to keep, especially at a time like that."

"I ain't lots of people. When it comes down to it, Bear, all a man's got is his word. I ain't never broken mine afore, and I'm not gonna start now. I'm fixing to stay put."

"I love you." The words slipped out of Bear's mouth

before he'd realized that they were forming on his lips. He froze, sucking his lip in between his teeth, his nerves starting to jangle like spurs on a hardwood floor, wondering how Pride was going to react to his sudden confession.

"Yeah? Well, that's good then, I guess, considering that I've loved you since the day I met you, for all that you're as prickly as a porcupine some days."

Bear let out a sigh of relief, not realizing that he'd been holding his breath. "I ain't prickly," he smiled, nuzzling Pride's neck, as a great wave of calm gently washed over him. His entire body relaxed and he felt a weight lift off his shoulders that he hadn't noticed he'd been carrying. Breathing deeply, he thought that he could lay there forever and not need a thing besides Pride's scent to sustain him.

"You are, too. Bristly as a hog on the wrong side of the fence from the trough," Pride grumbled, although his eyes were moist and his smile, tender. He pushed himself up, then leaned down for another kiss. "Now turn me loose, else that stew will burn. I've done worked up an appetite big enough for two, and burnt stew ain't what I'm hankering after."

Bear laughed softly, reluctantly letting Pride roll off of him. "Well, if I'm bristly, then it's only because you're as ornery as a polecat with a snout full of bramble thorns."

Pride grinned, lifting his hips and pulling his pants up. "Guess we're just the pair, ain't we? What say you make us some coffee while I get out the hardtack and tend to the stew, Bear."

Warmed to the toes knowing that Pride felt the same as he did, Bear grinned as he cleaned himself off and buttoned his fly. He got up and as he rummaged through their packs for the coffee grounds, he couldn't stop beaming. He was still grinning like a fool when the water boiled and he poured them both a cup. He smiled around his spoon as he shoveled in the stew, feeling it fill out his empty belly.

Could be that he'd never stop smiling again.

Chapter Eighteen

Pride had insisted that the crate of gold be stuffed into their tent with them. Having been robbed once before while he slept under the stars, he wasn't about to take any chances with their newfound wealth.

"Now, Pride... "

"Don't you '*now, Pride*' me, Bear. You wasn't the one that was conked over the head and left for dead while some lily-livered bastard stole everything you had in the world, now was you?"

Bear had no answer to that, and was too tired and happy to argue. He'd just rolled his eyes and helped Pride lug the box into their pup tent. Bear had spent most of the night curled up and twisted like a pretzel in the tight space. Still, somehow he'd managed to make it through the night, although he'd had tried to roll over a few times only to smack his head on the hard wood, growling something about a fool and his gold being soon parted.

His curses had gone unheard since Pride, being so much smaller than Bear, hadn't had any trouble at all and had slept like a baby all night.

When Bear awoke it was to birdsong, and the smell of strong coffee and frying bacon wafting in along with streams of bright sunshine through the flaps of the tent. Poking his head out of the tent, Bear realized that Pride must have risen with the sun and let him sleep in, because he had most of the campsite already packed up and waiting to go, and was busy making breakfast, frying up cornbread and bacon over the fire.

Bear smiled. A man could get used to being took care of like that. Pride never made a fuss about doing for Bear, neither. He was quiet about it, just seeing to Bear's needs without asking, and without expecting anything for it in return. Chiding himself silently for not saying thank you as often as he should, Bear hunkered down next to Pride and kissed his scruffy cheek. He accepted a piping hot cup of coffee from him, taking a sip and setting it down near the fire.

"Pride, you don't need to be doing all the work, you know."

"Ain't nothing. Besides, if I know you, you'll be toting that crate all the way home today and not letting me help at all. Least I can do is fix us some vittles and pack up."

"You're spoiling me, darlin'," Bear said, the endearment feeling good and coming as natural as breathing. He caught hold of Pride's chin and gave him a good and proper morning kiss before shuffling off into the brush to see to his morning needs.

Now, ain't that something.

Pride stared after Bear, a soft smile turning up his lips. *Darling*. Bear had called him *darling*. Nobody had ever called Pride a pet name before, not since his Ma had taken sick and died. *Sweet Pea* was what she'd called him when he was just knee high to a frog's eye. Nobody had *ever* called him *darling* before.

It felt good. No, better than good.

It felt *wonderful*, and gave Pride a warm and fuzzy feeling deep inside. For a moment he couldn't decide whether he wanted to laugh or cry or do both at the same time, and was sorely afraid he break down weeping and laughing like a loon.

He hadn't lied to Bear the night before, hadn't said the words just because he thought they were what Bear needed to hear. He'd meant them. Pride *was* home. And he knew in his heart that it wouldn't matter whether they lived out the rest of their days in Bear's cabin, in one of the fine old plantation houses Pride had seen during the war, or in a patched-up tent moving around the country like gypsies. No matter where they hung their hats, as long as Bear was with him, it would be home.

And he did love him. Lordy, how he loved that man. Knew it near from the start, from that horrible moment when he'd thought Bear had been shot dead. He thanked God every day that He'd seen fit to let Bear get winged instead of killed.

Darling.

Pride sighed and scraped the last of the bacon onto Bear's plate. Sitting back with his coffee, he wondered what he should call Bear. Seemed only right that if Bear were going to call Pride by a pet name, that Pride should return the favor. What did a man call somebody as big as Bear? *Darlin'* was taken and *Sweetheart* didn't sound right. *Dear* didn't fit him, neither. *Honey*? Nah, sounded too girly for a man as big and burly as Bear. *Sugar? Lover?* Definitely not *Sweet Pea*. Nothing sounded right to him.

Movement in the bushes caught his attention as Bear walked back into the campsite and settled himself down next to Pride, picking up his plate and digging in. Pride, sipping his coffee, watched Bear eat for a while, and thought about everything Bear had come to mean to him.

The one thing Pride knew without a doubt was that he wouldn't be alive today if it hadn't been for Bear. He'd have died tied to that tree, supper for the mountain lion that Bear had shot, and the world would have never been the wiser. He'd have been dead, and no one would have cared a lick.

Truth was that Pride hadn't really felt alive since the night his pa had taken the strop to his back, not until Bear had taken him in, accepted him, loved him. He'd saved Pride's life in more ways than one, Pride realized.

If Pride had a Guardian Angel, then his name was *Bear*.

Pride started, then smiled. That was it. That sounded right to him, said everything he felt about Bear in a single word. *Angel*.

Taking Bear's plate, he quickly scraped and cleaned the dishes, packing them up, then went to work on the tent.

Between the two of them they had the campsite knocked down and packed up in no time, especially since Pride had done as much as possible before Bear had even woken up. Shouldering the knapsack, he smiled up at Bear. "Ready, angel?"

"*Angel?*" Bear smirked, grunting as he lifted the heavy crate of gold onto his broad shoulders. "Ain't I too big and hairy to be an angel?"

"Nope. You're my angel, and that's all there is to it, Bear," Pride replied, winking at him. "An angel with horns sometimes, sure enough, but an angel just the same. And you make living on earth pure heaven, as far as I'm concerned."

Bear didn't say anything else, just started walking, but Pride could swear that his eyes glistened as he passed by.

They'd stopped several times over the course of the day to rest, to allow Bear to sit down his burden and stretch his sore muscles. Being Bear, he'd proven Pride correct and hadn't allowed him to touch the crate, let alone try to carry it.

"Don't be stupid, Pride. This here thing weighs in as much as you do, if not more. You can't carry it."

"Are you *trying* to piss me off, or are you just getting lucky? I'm not some piece of dainty china bric-a-brac, Bear. I'm not gonna break, and I'm stronger than I look. Give me that damned thing for a while!" Pride growled, fixing Bear with a look that might have made a lesser man squirm.

Luckily for Bear, he wasn't a lesser man.

"No. Now, just keep your dagger eyes to yourself. You don't scare me none, and I ain't gonna let you tear yourself up inside just to prove that you can tote this thing. Let it be, Pride," Bear said, glaring down at Pride with a look of his own that wouldn't have made a lesser man squirm – it would have loosened his bowels.

Unfortunately for Bear, Pride wasn't a lesser man either.

"You're grating on my very last nerve, Bear. Ain't no reason for me not to take a turn carrying that box, except if it's that you don't trust me with it," Pride grumbled, his eyes flashing with sparks of anger. "You done said that the treasure was half mine. Well, I want to carry my half!"

"Now, the problem we got us is that *your* half is stuck up in here with *my* half, and I ain't letting go of my half," Bear chuckled, despite the fierce looks Pride was shooting up at him. "When we get home you can tote your half around the cabin, if it'll make you feel better."

"Bear, I swear you are the most goddamn stubborn, pigheaded, mulish--"

"I know, I know...old goat," Bear said, still chuckling.

"...that I have ever locked horns with in all my born days!" Pride finished, as if Bear hadn't interrupted him. "And it's a damn good thing that I love you, else I'd be fixing to tear you up one side and the down the other right about now, Bear."

"Now that would be a sight, wouldn't it?" Bear grinned. "'Specially since you'd need a ladder to get over the top of me."

Pride paused, staring slack-jawed up at Bear for a moment, then burst into laughter. "Guess you're right, at that, seeing how God must've had leftovers from making other men and used every last scrap He had, plus some, to make you, Bear."

"Looky here. We're nearly home, Pride. The cabin is just through that thicket yonder," Bear said, nodding toward a thick copse of juniper.

They broached the tree line, entering the clearing just as the sunset began to paint the sky in reds and purples, and both sighed with relief when the cabin sprang into view. But as they neared it, a cold tingle touched Bear's spine. He stopped in his tracks, lowering the crate to the ground.

"Pride," he whispered, "Gimme my shotgun."

"What's wrong, Bear?" Pride asked, not letting go of the stock of the gun. He kept it cradled under his arm, frowning in the direction Bear was staring.

"The door's open. I *never* leave it open. All manner of critters would go in, make themselves to home, tear the place up," Bear hissed, keeping his voice low.

"Think maybe one of them opened it? 'Coons can be pretty damned smart. Bears, too."

"'Coons might be smart enough to unhook a latch, Pride, but they'd never reach it. A bear would likely just batter the door down if they wanted in bad enough."

"I'm keeping the shotgun. I'm a better shot than you," Pride insisted when Bear tried to take the gun from him.

"The *hell* you say. This ain't the time to be contrary, Pride. Give it over."

"No."

"Goddamn it, Pride!"

"Shh...you want whoever's inside to know that we're home?"

"It's my goddamn gun! Give it up, now," Bear hissed, yanking the shotgun out from under Pride's arm and ignoring the blue streak Pride cursed at him from under his breath. He cocked it, then started for the cabin. "You stay here, Pride. You ain't armed."

"Bullshit. I'm not staying behind. That's my home, too, Bear."

As angry as Bear was for being disobeyed, and as fearful as he was that Pride might get hurt, his words still warmed him. "Well then, stay behind me and keep your head low."

"No, I thought I'd jump up and down in front of the window so I'd make an easier target," Pride sniffed sarcastically. "I'm not an idiot, Bear."

"Then quit acting like one and stay behind me." Bear wasn't in the mood for jokes, not when there was an uninvited stranger with unknown intentions bunkered down in their cabin. He crept along, half bent over, keeping to the side of the cabin where he was less likely to be seen if someone was watching for their return.

Creeping around the side of the cabin onto the porch, wincing every time his foot creaked on a floorboard, Bear ducked under the window and flattened himself to the side of the doorway, holding the shotgun in both hands, ready to fire. Pride stood next to him, on just the other side of the window. He'd pulled the kitchen knife from their knapsack, and held it ready. Together they waited, senses alert, listening hard to pick up any sound from inside.

"Hello? Who's in there?" Bear called, tensing. He half expected a full out attack, but none came.

It was as silent as the grave inside, but Bear knew that that meant little. Could be whoever was in there didn't want to give themselves away until they could get a clear shot. Whoever it was, they were either dead or meant him and Pride ill, else they would've answered him by now.

"Who are you? Come out here where I can see you!" he called, his finger tightening on the trigger of the shotgun.

Chapter Nineteen

"You know who I am!" a voice rang out. It was unfamiliar, but there was bitterness in it, and so much hate that it tickled Bear's spine like a cold, dead finger. "Come inside, Bear! I've been waiting for you, you bastard!"

"Who are you?" Bear hollered back. He exchanged a look with Pride and shrugged his shoulders. He didn't have the slightest clue who the man might be, or how he knew Bear. "I don't recall your voice."

The man cackled madly. "You know me. Been fifteen years, but I ain't never forgot *you*, you fucker! You killed my daddy! Remember that, Bear? Waltzed right up to our front porch and shot him clean between the eyes. Now do you know who I am?"

Bear paused a minute, his gut twisting as he let painful memories from the past bubble to the surface, bringing a name with them. "Zack?"

"That's me, asshole! I knew you'd remember me. Come to pay you back for killing my pa. Waited fifteen fucking years for this moment. Now come in here and face me like a man. I wanna see your eyes when you die, Bear."

"Ain't gonna do that, Zack. 'Sides, your pa had it coming. Killed my whole family, the worthless bastard. He shot my baby sister in her fucking cradle! Killed my ma and left her lying facedown in the mud! My brothers too, and branded my pa like he was nothing more than an animal! He deserved what he got and more," Bear bellowed, his muscles clenching with the same anger and grief he'd felt all those years ago. He twitched in the direction of the door, but Pride's hand stayed him.

"Don't be a fool, Bear," Pride hissed. "He'll shoot you before you can cross the threshold. He's trying to get you riled up so you'll make a stupid mistake."

Bear nodded, taking a deep breath to calm him. "What's done is done, Zack. Blood was spilled on both sides. We're even," Bear called. "Now, come on out."

"Even? *Even?*" Zack cried, as something heavy banged against the window shutters. The skillet, maybe, Bear thought. "Not nearly! Not until you've got a bullet hole right between your eyes, Bear! Not until you're dead and the vultures are picking at your bones! Not until the Devil himself is dancing a jig over your worthless soul!"

A shot rang out, chipping a splinter from the doorjamb, perilously close to Bear's ear.

Bear decided to try another tack. "You're right, Zack. I was wrong to do what I done. Should've let the sheriff handle it. Come on out now, and I'll go with you back to Abilene, let the law decide what's to be done."

"The law? The *law* tried to string me up! Yeah, that's right. Your good friend the sheriff said I was guilty of murder, same as you, Bear. 'Cept he didn't give me a chance to clear out like he done you. If my daddy's men hadn't busted me out of jail, I'd have swung." Zack cackled, and the sound of madness froze Bear's blood. "And why? Just for obeying my pa, that's why. For being a good son! Got him good though. He swung instead of me, on the end of the very rope they was gonna tie around my neck!"

"What?" Bear shook his head, tossing Pride a puzzled look. "You killed the sheriff? Why were they gonna hang you, Zack?"

"Man, ain't you just as thick as a block of wood! Did you really think my *pa* shot your worthless family? He was a busy man, Bear, an *important* man. He didn't have time to do it himself. Told me to do it. And I did! But he was pissed because you wasn't there. Said I had to get you, too, or else we couldn't claim the land. But I never got the chance to kill you. Not until now."

"*You*? You killed them?" Bear was floored. He felt his stomach sink to his feet as a new fear clenched at his innards. All those years... All those years of thinking that he'd done right, that he'd avenged his family... Had he killed an innocent man? Was he no better than his family's murderer? How could he live with himself if that were true? Slumping back against the wall of the cabin, he slowly lowered his gun as guilt washed over him.

"Don't you listen to him, Bear. He's just trying to confuse you," Pride whispered. "Even if it's true, his pa still gave the order. That makes him just as guilty as if he'd pulled the trigger, Bear."

"Who's that?" Zack called. "That your little whore you got with you, Bear? Been fucking him all winter? Goddamn sodomizing bastard. Should've slit his throat while I him tied to the tree! He killed Levi and fucked up my arm! Well, I got a bullet with his name on it, too."

"That was *you* that jumped me?" Pride yelled, turning toward the door. "*You* that shot Bear? You almost fucking killed him! Come out here, you coward!"

"Wish I *did* kill him that day! Would've saved me a heap of trouble. Should've died back with the rest of his family anyway. Hey, Bear! Did you know that your ma died begging for her baby's life? That I shot your pa in the back? Got your brothers while they was running to your ma. Shit, it was like shooting fish in a barrel, I swear! I gave your sister her little rag doll before I killed her. She was a sweet little thing, too. Smiling and cooing right up until the minute I put a bullet in her."

Bear screamed then. He couldn't see, couldn't hear; couldn't feel anything except for the thick, choking black rage that swept over him. Fury like he'd never felt before boiled up from his gut, a tornado of misery that he'd kept bottled up for fifteen years. Set free, it blinded him to everything except one fact: the man who'd killed his family in cold blood, who'd stolen everything from him and left him to wander alone was sitting right there, just a few feet away.

In one swift movement, Bear turned and pushed the door open fully, firing a shot wildly into the room. He heard a pop, and felt air rush past his ear even as he was falling.

Pride screamed along with Bear, but not for the same reason. He saw Bear tense and move, and was reaching for him even as Bear kicked open the door. Tackling Bear around the knees, he brought him down hard. Shots rang out, one clipping the back of Pride's left thigh, although he barely felt it. Instead, he acted instinctively, grabbing Bear's shotgun and cocking it, firing it into the cabin in the direction the shots had come from.

A shriek pierced the air, and a few more wild shots ricocheted around the cabin. Pride bent low over Bear, covering him with his body until the last *pinging* sound died away and everything fell silent again.

Straddling Bear's back, Pride fished a shell out of Bear's pocket with trembling fingers and cracked open the shotgun, slipped it into the chamber, and took another shot at Zack. The sound of the blast made his ears ring, but he breathed easier when there was no return fire.

Bear tried to shrug Pride off, but Pride refused to budge until he'd assured himself that Bear wasn't hurt. He ran his fingers over Bear's scalp, petrified that they'd come away bloody.

"Get off me, Pride!" Bear thundered. "I'm going to kill that bastard!"

"Too late, Bear. I think I did it for you," Pride said, sighing in relief when his fingers came away clean. He felt the stinging pain in his thigh, but kept it to himself. Bear was too keyed up – knowing Pride had been hurt would only make matters worse. Besides, from the feel of it, Pride reckoned it was only a scratch anyway.

Pride grabbed a couple of shells from Bear's pocket and stood up, favoring his left leg. He had the shotgun reloaded and cocked, and was inside the cabin before Bear could rise up off the porch.

A man sat on the floor in the corner near the fireplace, half-slumped over. Pride lowered the shotgun when he realized that Zack was no longer a threat. Having goodly portion of your head blasted all over the wall tended to make a man a mite easier to get along with. Damn, Pride thought, it's gonna take a while to clean up *that* mess.

"Shit," Bear said, walking in behind Pride. "Bastard killed them all, Pride, my whole family. And I killed the wrong man in return." His voice was etched with pain and guilt, and Pride ached for him.

"No, you didn't. You heard what he said, Bear. His father gave him orders to do it. He wasn't any less guilty than Zack, and now they're both dead. Let it go, Bear," he said softly, reaching for him.

"You know what kind of hate makes a man hunt somebody for so many years?" Bear asked, staring at Zack's bloody remains. "I know what it feels like to hate like that. I killed his pa and still spent the next fifteen years hating him. It hurts, Pride. It eats at you until you're empty inside. Me and him," Bear whispered, nodding toward Zack, "We're the same."

"The *hell* you are! He was crazy, Bear. He was as mean as a rattler, and a coward, too. Sneaking up on people while they're asleep! Shooting men in the back! Killing helpless children!" Pride pushed himself away from Bear, glaring up at him. "That ain't you, Bear. You did what you had to do and moved on. You ain't hurt a soul since then."

"I ran away, instead of standing like a man and facing a judge. I'm a coward, Pride," Bear said, staring at Zack's body. "Lord, I shouldn't have listened to the sheriff. He's dead because of me, too. His blood's on my hands, too."

"No, it ain't. You didn't kill the sheriff – Zack did. You saved my life, Bear! Do you think Zack or his daddy would've done that? He's the one who tied me up and left me to die in the first place! No, Bear. If you hadn't left home when you did, I'd be dead now." Wrapping his arms around Bear's waist, Pride held him as tightly as he could.

Bear was eerily silent, staring over the top of Pride's head toward the body that sagged in the corner of the cabin. He didn't hug Pride back, his arms hanging limply at his sides. Pride bit his lip, looking up at Bear's grief-stricken face. It was going to take some doing to bring him around and make him think about something other than his sorrow, and Pride sighed and rolled his eyes, knowing exactly what would do it.

"Um, Bear?"

Bear didn't answer. Didn't so much as flinch, and Pride worried that he wouldn't be able to reach him after all. "Bear? I'm hurt."

Bear's eyes blinked, then flicked down toward Pride,

frowning. "What? What did you say?"

"I said that I believe I've been shot. Not bad," Pride hastened to say when Bear's eyes went wide and his face lost all its color. "Just a scratch, but... "

"Shit. If he wasn't dead already I'd kill him," Bear snarled, looking over at Zack's body. He spat, hitting the dead man's boots. Looking back down at Pride, he asked, "Where?"

"In the leg," Pride answered, twisting to look at the back of his thigh. "Ain't much, but it should be cleaned and--"

He didn't finish his thought. Bear scooped him up in his arms as if he weighed no more than a feather, and carried him into the alcove, setting him down gently on the bed. "Don't you move, Pride. You let me do all the work."

"It ain't but a scratch, Bear--"

"Hush up, now! Just let me work. Gonna fix you up, then I got some cleaning to do," he grumbled, nodding toward the main room of the cabin.

"I can do that, Bear. You don't need to be seeing him again." But one black look from Bear was all it took to still Pride's tongue. This was what Bear needed to heal, he thought. Needed to see to Pride, then needed to bury the past. "Hey," Pride called softly, sitting up and reaching for Bear.

Bear sunk down next to him, lowering his head so that Pride could reach his lips. He kissed Bear softly, feeling his love for the man well up and overflow. Wrapping his arms around his neck, he held Bear for a while, rocking gently back and forth, until Bear finally pulled away and smiled weakly at him.

"Let's get you tended to, Pride," he said, laying him back down and setting to work on his shirt buttons. He gently eased Pride's clothes off, then urged him to roll over onto his stomach.

"Don't look too serious, Pride. Just a gash, and not too deep at that. Gonna go get the jug. Be right back," Bear said as he ran his finger gently around the area of Pride's thigh that had been wounded, about six inches below his left butt cheek.

"Oh, Lordy, Bear... "

Bear snorted. "What goes around, comes around, Pride. Let me think, what was it you said when you was fixing to torture me when I was shot? Oh, yeah. *Wouldn't hurt you lest I had to, Bear,*" Bear mimicked in a trembling falsetto voice. He cracked a small smile as Pride grimaced.

"I don't sound like that, Bear. You make me sound like a woman!"

"You'll be screamin' like one once I take the whiskey to your hide," Bear chuckled. "I remember that sting, and let me tell you boy, it ain't fun. No, sir. Not in the least bit."

"You're taking too much pleasure in this, Bear," Pride grumbled, although he was secretly pleased to see the light back in Bear's eyes and a smile on his handsome face. He'd take the burning pain of alcohol on an open wound any day if it meant making Bear smile and forget his troubles for a piece.

And burn it did – like the very fires of Hell. Pride hissed and bit down hard on the pillow to keep from screeching when the alcohol hit the bullet scratch. "Are you *laughing*, Bear?"

"Me? Nah. You're hearing things."

"Yeah, I am. And what I hear sounds like you laughing."

"Sit still," Bear said, slapping Pride lightly on the ass. "I'm gonna bandage it up, then see to the mess we got in the other room."

"You sure you don't want me to help you, Bear? You

don't have to do this alone."

"I know it, and I appreciate it, Pride. Surely I do. But I'd rather do this myself. I think I *need* to do it alone. Get rid of the ghosts once and for all," Bear said softly.

Pride nodded, rolling to his side after Bear finished tying off the edges of a makeshift bandage he'd ripped from the hem of his shirt. He studied Bear with worried eyes. "You gonna be all right?"

"Yeah. He just took me by surprise, is all. I'm sorry you got dragged into my mess, Pride. If he wasn't looking for me, he wouldn't have come across you and knocked you out, taken your things."

"I'm not. If he hadn't, I never would have met you," Pride said softly. "Everything happens for a reason, Bear. What we got together is worth a helluva lot more than a bump on the noggin or a scratch on the ass."

"Ain't your ass that's scratched. It's your thigh. And if you think that I'm letting you out of bed afore it's healed, you got another think coming."

"Don't be silly, Bear! It's not like I took a bullet like you did... "

"Will you *please* hush up and let me take care of you for a change? You done coddled me when I was hurt. It's my turn now."

Pride smiled as Bear turned away. He lay back against the pillow and staring at the wood beam ceiling, listening to the thumps and clatters Bear was making in the main room.

Pride couldn't barely remember the last time he'd had anybody in his life that had given a good goddamn about whether he lived or died. He was still thinking about the warm feeling it gave him when his eyes fluttered closed and he drifted off into an exhausted sleep.

Pride awoke sometime during the night, feeling the edge of the bed dip down as Bear lowered himself to stretch out beside him. He rolled over, resting his head on Bear's chest and sliding an arm around his waist. "You okay?" he whispered, looking up at Bear's shadowed face.

"Yeah. Dragged his sorry ass out into the woods and buried him. I'll whittle out a marker tomorrow."

"That's more than he deserved, Bear. Should've just thrown his body to the crows."

Bear shook his head, his eyes closed and his brows knit. "No. That wouldn't be right, Pride. Just because he was lower than a snake don't mean I need to be. He was a man, and even though he was a thieving, murdering, *bastard* of a man, he deserves to be buried like one."

"You're a saint, Bear. That's what you are. A fucking saint."

"A saint? Me? I doubt it, but if I am then I'm a tired one, that's for sure. Plum tuckered out," Bear yawned, his jaws popping. "Been a helluva day, darlin'." He slipped an arm under Pride's shoulders, tucking him in close, and was asleep with his next breath.

Chapter Twenty

Bear dreamt that he was fucking Pride, riding him hard on a solid gold bed that sat atop Zack's makeshift grave, when he suddenly awoke to find himself with more than a simple morning erection. He looked down to see Pride's blond head bobbing over his groin.

"Thought I told you to rest that leg," he growled, rocking his hips up a bit, the dream already forgotten as he bent and spread his knees for Pride's slick fingers.

Pride let go only long enough to flash him a brief smile. "Do I look like I'm dancing a jig? I'm laying here, same as you." Teasingly, he swiped his tongue up along the length of Bear's cock, ending with a flick over the head.

"It ain't the same thing. Oh, Lord, Pride..." Bear moaned, as Pride's fingers found his asshole and slipped deep inside him. They moved with the same rhythm as Pride's lips, sending bolts of pleasure sizzling through Bear's body. In, out, up, down. Again. Again. Faster.

As he began to ride Pride's fingers, developing an easy rhythm between Pride's lips and hand, sweet tension began to stir in Bear's balls. It was like this whenever Pride touched him. Never failed to bring Bear to the edge as fast as greased lightning, his balls swelling up and his cock growing hard enough to split wood. "Gonna do it soon, Pride," he gasped, threading his fingers into Pride's hair. "Gonna come, darlin'."

"Oh, no, angel. Not without me, you ain't," Pride grinned. He pulled away and pushed at Bear's hip, urging him onto his side. Rolling over, Bear felt Pride's fingers pry apart his cheeks, and then the familiar, burning fullness as Pride pushed himself inside Bear's body. Lordy, what that man did to him! Made him want to curse Pride and bless him at the same time; to push him away because the pleasure was too much to bear, and beg him for more with the same breath.

"Bear," Pride groaned, his hips slapping hard against Bear's ass as he drove himself in deeper, "Do it, Bear. I can't hold on much longer. You first, angel." The fingers of one hand dug into Bear's hip while his other hand fisted in Bear's hair, pulling his head back. "Do it now, boy! Now!"

"Pride!" Bear yelled, his hand working furiously over his cock. He came good and hard, painting a white trail across the patchwork quilt. His ass clenched tightly as Pride emptied himself into Bear's body, liquid fire filling him up to the brim.

After a few moments of lying sated and gasping for air like a pair of dying fish, Pride pulled out and away. He nuzzled Bear's neck for a moment before getting out of bed, leaving Bear dripping from both ends. Bear sighed contentedly, swinging his legs over the side of the mattress. What a truly wonderful way to start the morning. What was even better was that Pride was almost always agreeable to starting everyday this way, and was usually up for ending it in a similar fashion. Been that way for the past week, ever since they'd come home and found Zack waiting for them.

Bear still felt a powerful tug in his chest when he thought about Zack, because it never failed to remind him of his family. Shrugging it off, he ambled into the kitchen and out the front door, still stark naked, to join Pride as he peed off the front porch. With Pride around, Bear found that it was becoming easier to set aside the pain and remember his family fondly. He thought of that as one of the greatest gifts Pride had given him.

"Flapjacks for breakfast?" Pride asked, giving his dick a shake and padding back into the cabin with Bear not far behind.

"I'll fix 'em. You're supposed to be resting," Bear growled. "You start that gash a-bleeding again, and I'll be on you like flies on shit, Pride."

"Oh, quit nagging on me. I'm nearly healed," Pride answered, waving his hand at Bear as if he were an annoying mosquito. "It was only a scratch. A body would think I'd had my leg shot off, the way you've been carrying on."

"No worse than you did me when I was shot."

"Bullshit. I didn't have a bullet stuck in me. All it did was kiss my ass on its way out the door." Nevertheless, he sat down at the table as Bear went about the business of making breakfast.

Sitting down to flapjacks and coffee, Bear nodded toward the box of gold ingots that decorated one corner of the cabin.

There had been 1,752 of the small lumps of gold in the box they'd dug up. Near as Bear and Pride could figure, that translated into more money than either of them had ever before seen lumped together in one place.

"So...what are we going to do with it all?" Bear asked around a mouthful of honey-soaked flapjacks.

Pride sipped his coffee and wrinkled his nose, reaching for the sugar. "Don't know. I guess we could go into St.

Elmo's and buy something."

"Buy what?"

"Whatever we want, I reckon."

"Ain't nothing I need, 'cept a new Bowie."

"Then we buy you a new Bowie. I need a few things, too. Clothes, a rifle...although I think maybe I'd rather have a pair of revolvers."

Bear nodded, chewing and swallowing his last forkful. "Pride?"

"Yeah?"

"How about we take that trip you was talking about? Go see the ocean like you wanted."

"You mean it?" Pride asked as his eyes lit up like a small boy on Christmas morning.

"Sure, I mean it. Ain't nothing keeping us here. It's late enough in the season to cross the mountains. Pass ought to be clear by now."

"That sounds like a mighty fine plan, Bear," Pride smiled, slapping his palm against his knee. "We can head down to St. Elmo's, buy what we need, and hit the trail."

Bear sat back in his chair, looking around the cabin. "It's going to feel a mite funny, leaving this place. Been my home for so long now."

"We'll be coming back, Bear."

"I reckon. Never can tell, though. Besides, it don't really matter none. It's just a cabin. We can always build another one someplace else," Bear said, looking at Pride. He reached over the table and lightly stroked the back of Pride's hand. "It ain't the cabin that makes a home. It's them that lives inside it."

Pride felt his eyes mist, and he jumped up and bustled to the stove, getting them more coffee before he broke, put his head down and wept right there in his flapjacks. Home. Up until Pride had met Bear, *home* had been a dirty word that Pride had uttered like a curse. *Home* had meant pain and loss, hate and lonely silence. Now, in the space of a few months, it had changed into somewhere Pride would fight tooth and nail to be.

As Pride watched, Bear padded naked into the alcove, searching for his woolens at the foot of the bed where they'd been thrown the night before. He realized that it didn't matter to him whether Bear wanted to travel to California, New York, or Katmandu. Pride would be right there with him, dogging his footsteps because Bear had changed the meaning of another word for Pride.

Friend.

Since that night in the barn when he'd been fourteen, Pride had known men, had fucked them from time to time, had watched them die alongside him in battle, had ridden long hours with them on the ranch, but he'd never been friends with any of them. Friendship, Pride had learned at an early age, brought pain.

Not Bear's friendship. Oh, it wasn't always pretty, and that was a fact. They argued, like friends do from time to time. Won some, lost some, pouted and stormed some, but in the end they were still always friends.

He smiled when Bear straightened up, triumphantly clutching his long johns in his hand. Yeah, Pride loved that big ol' ox. He picked up his coffee cup, watching Bear over the rim and thinking about how funny life worked out sometimes. How unexpected twists and turns in the path a man walked brought him to places he'd never have gone otherwise.

Ain't that always the way.

Kiernan Kelly

In Bear Country

Made in the USA
Monee, IL
27 August 2025

24435110R00105